THE FANTASY MASTER

By G.L. Henderson

Revised

Published in the USA by
Conquering Books, LLC
210 E. Arrowhead Drive, Suite #1
Charlotte, NC 28213
(704) 509-2226

Third Edition – Third Printing
May 2005

This book is a work of fiction.
Places, events, and situations in this story
are purely fictional. Any resemblance to actual persons, living or dead is   coincidental.

ISBN: 1-4140-2414-2 (e-book)
ISBN: 1-4140-2415-0 (Paperback)
ISBN: 1-4140-7410-7 (Dust Jacket)

TABLE OF CONTENTS

Acknowledgements

I first acknowledge you God for loving me the way you do. Even in the mist of my wrong doings, you still chose to bless me. This little message can't possibly be enough to say thank you. So I will use this gift to spread your precious name and the outcome of what happens when you visit late in the midnight hour.

To my mothers Edith Henderson and Mary A. Sims thank you for your endless support, with all my faults it takes a mother to not notice them. I want to say I love you with all my heart and soul. To my daughter Camerie and Goddaughter NiNi although you are too young to read this, I want you to know that I love you more than words can ever say. All of this is for you. I love you both.

To little Greg I can't make up for lost time, but I want you to know that I love you and I am always thinking of you. To the Henderson, Sims and Greathouse families, thanks for all the support.

A very special thanks to Charlene Pearson (my baby mama...lol) thank you for being there and for being a real Godmother to Cam. Nana I thank you for your support also. I didn't know, when I got Charlene as Cam's godmother, I was getting two for the price of one.

Special thanks: Apostle James Hartsfield and Pastor Lenora Hartsfield, Wilmo Management, my tour partner and label mate Shyan and family (check her cd out "It's About Time"). Ty and Cee Springfield (for your help keeping me sane), Jaquee Hudson. Army Chaplain School Staff (you'll know who you are). U.S Army Recruiting Staff (too many to name). Mrs. Perry and Dentac staff (Ft. Jackson, SC), Wesley (AAFES, SC), Jonathon Fant, Johnnie Greene and Jackie for giving me a chance to be on your BET Comicview tour.

Thank you South Carolina for embracing me as one of your own. (Columbia, Orangeburg, Florence, Sumter and Camden)

"On the path of trying to achieve my goals, I lost many people whom I thought would endure to the end with me. I made some bad choices as well as some good ones, but I had to do what I had to. Those of you that misunderstood some of my actions, I prayed that you'd hang in there to see that things wasn't the way they appeared. During this struggle if I have offended, hurt or disrespected any one, I apologize. I pray that God continues to bless us all."

G.L.

**In loving memory of my brother, best-friend and partner.
Lester Tisdale
(1967-2004)**

Dedication

This book is dedicated to the ones I've
lost and loved
I know you're watching me from the sky
above
I thank you for all the times we shared
on earth
I thank you grandma for loving me from
birth
To my brothers Lester and Fred I miss
you so much
I know you're protecting me, I can feel
your touch
Auntie and uncle I didn't get a chance to
tell you before you passed
I love you both, I know you're together
on heaven's grass
Aunt Ida Mae I miss your laughter and
smile
I know being in heaven made it all worth
while
Big Momma Sims my pride and joy
You watched me turn into a man from a
boy
I know you wanted to see the finished
book

I know you're peeping over me taking a
look
I love you all and I miss you very much
When you're walking next to God, ask
him to give me a touch
When I'm down on my knees ask him to
lift me
Ask him to spare me, so I can reach my
destiny

CHAPTER 1

Jasmine awoke covered in sweat. Her hair that was once covered by a red satin wrap now lay moist on her shoulders. Her bloodshot eyes surrounded her light brown pupils, like the dark sky to a lonely moon. Her heartbeat was rapid, like a drum at an African ritual. She tossed the blanket to the side, allowing the cool air to help simmer her body temperature. Her hands moved smoothly across her wet skin, wiping the sweat from her brow. She climbed out of bed turned and looked at her wet navy blue satin sheets. She dreamt of a passionate encounter, one that took her every fear and turned them into one erotic journey. A journey that made her inner passions come to life, some she never even knew existed.

She peeped over at Lewis lying there motionless. She nudged him just enough to see if he'd awaken, but he hadn't. Jasmine needed to confide in someone about what she had experienced. Her girlfriend Renee was the first to come to mind. The two had grown up in a small town near Montgomery, Alabama. They use to sit up many long nights, discussing their adolescent issues. She knew at this moment no one but Renee would understand.

She quietly walked down the dark hallway, to the dimly lit living room. She grabbed the cordless phone, still in disbelief about what she had dreamt. Jasmine curled up tightly on her leather chair and dialed Renee. She anxiously waited for her girlfriend to pick-up. She anticipated hearing Renee's voice, but she was greeted by a recording.

"Renee, are you there?" she softly spoke into her machine, trying not to wake Lewis. Picking up the phone Renee responded, "Yes I'm here, what's wrong?" she said as she caught her breath.

"I have to tell you about a dream I had. It seemed so real," Jasmine said. She began telling her about the dream. Renee couldn't believe her ears.

"It all seemed too real," Jasmine said.

"Are you sure it didn't happen for real and you're covering up an actual encounter with this dream? Did you really meet a guy like that? Come on Jazz you can tell me!"

"No! But I wish Lewis was that guy," she said humorously.

"So what's the problem?" Renee asked.

"I feel bad dreaming about another guy. I could actually feel his breath on me, that scared me. I love Lewis despite all his faults and mistakes, but he needs to appreciate me more. I know we're having problems, but every relationship does. I'm just tired of always feeling like I've done something wrong, when I know I didn't do anything. I just hope he's not looking elsewhere for love. I pray the dream wasn't a sign that Lewis is not the one for me."

"Don't be silly Jasmine, that boy loves you. Trust me I know. Besides, who else is going to put up with his mess," Renee responded. They continued laughing and joking about Lewis and finally hung up the phone.

She headed back to her room, stood over the bed looking at Lewis. "I hope I'm all you need," Jasmine mumbled under her breath. She sat on her bed for a moment, thinking about the conversation she had with Renee.

"Maybe she's right. He does love me and only me, so why am I doubting myself?" She crawled into bed, snuggled next to Lewis and drifted back to sleep.

Jasmine is a woman considered by most men to be very beautiful. She has all the right parts in all the right places. She's a catch, a man's arm trophy, a woman to be desired in the bedroom. She could grace the cover of any magazine; she's always being mistaken for a model or an actress. She has a good head on her shoulders. She's independent and beautiful, a combination most men fear. Jasmine, like many modern day women, had been hurt and now she's in her healing phase; the recovery zone. It's that phase where most men stand no chance at all in breaking through the barriers.

Jasmine was coming out of a relationship where her trust was violated. She was involved with Lewis. He was a guy she met through Renee. They met about two years ago on a double date with Renee and her then boyfriend Sam. They hit it off very well; they started as friends, and then became lovers. Lewis would always bring her flowers, open her car door and do any little thing that would make her smile. He would even pull her chair out when they sat down to eat. Then like most relationships, things began to go sour. They began to have arguments, periods of no conversations and the bedroom was more suitable for a study hall. The flowers stopped and the little things stopped and soon the romance stopped.

Lewis was an average looking man. He was slim in build, a clean-cut gentleman. When he walked around with Jasmine, he would make his chest swell, trying to give the impression that he was bigger than he was. Lewis was employed by the government as a contractor for an electric company. He had strange hours and was always on call, but he used to make all his time with Jasmine count. His love for her was there, but something was missing. Communication was the last thing on their to do list and the lack of that was causing their relationship to suffer. Now he was always tired when he came home, always finding excuses to argue.

Despite the problems, Jasmine continued doing the little things; cooking, preparing his bath water and she always had on something sexy for him when he came home. She would get her hair and nails done and buy something seductive from the lingerie store. Knowing that he would be tired when he arrived, this would help take his mind off things. She knew what he needed and she was willing to do what she could to please him, but she had limitations. Lewis had strong sexual desires and was always asking Jasmine to try different things. She felt some of his choices were reasonable, but lately they started getting out of hand. Soon all those requests stopped coming. He would come home and dismiss the beautiful sight in front of him. He was now too tired to do anything and would go straight to bed. Jasmine couldn't take it any more. She decided one night to not put on anything sexy and see if that would catch his attention. She tried throwing herself at him in the bed, but rejection was all she got. The once passionate kisses became pecks and the long bear hugs became friendship hugs. She wondered if his job had become his lover or was someone at his job loving him. Jasmine started looking at herself and wondered if there was something wrong with her. With thoughts like that, she knew she had to talk to him and there would be no better time than the present.

She confronted Lewis the next evening when he came home. "Lewis, my dear, how was work?" she asked.

"Same ole', same ole'. I can't complain. Why?" he responded.

"Well I'm worried about you, I mean I'm worried about us," she said boldly.

"What is there to be concerned about, I thought we were doing fine," he responded with a blank look.

"Fine! You think we're doing fine? Since you wanna be ignant, let me help you. Let's see hmm! We haven't had sex, made love, screwed or any of the above in three weeks. You don't hold me in the bed, your kisses are different, and you're coming home late every evening. Hell! Lewis you don't even hold my hand in public, like you used to. I would say something's wrong here," she said sarcastically.

"It's nothing baby. I've been stressed out at work and things are just now balancing out. I'm sorry that I have been neglecting you. I'll make it up to you, I promise," he said as he tried to hug her. Jasmine backed away from him, stared into his eyes and said, "You just said a minute ago, that things at work were great and you couldn't be happier, so which is it? Lewis, eyes tell more than you think and I want you to know that I love you more than I can ever express, but I am no one's fool."

Lewis smirked and said, "Baby, you don't have to worry about a thing, everything is going to be alright."

"Don't let this conversation go in one ear and out the other. If you hurt me, I'll never forgive you," she said in a serious tone.

That night everything seemed awkward as they prepared for bed and their conversations were non-existing. Jasmine rolled over and knew what she was feeling wasn't good. She felt her heart racing and sickness in her stomach. Her head began pounding; she got up and took two aspirins, hoping they would help ease the pain brewing in her head. She checked the bandage on her back, making sure it was secured. She said her prayer, then made her way into bed. She didn't want to push it with him, so she pulled the covers close and dozed off to sleep. Lewis climbed in shortly after; slowly he began to press his body next to hers. Tears began to trickle down her cheek as she lay on her side, looking at the wall. His fire was turned on by the aggression she displayed, but those flames were quickly extinguished.

"Lewis! I'm not in the mood. You know what?"

"What?"

"Why don't you go sleep in the spare bed," she said as she moved away from him.

"You go sleep in it," he said as he giggled.

"I will," she said as she threw the sheets off her, leaving the bed.

"Don't leave. I was joking Jazz."

"Well I hope you find this funny!" she said slamming the door behind her.

"Fine leave!" he yelled.

The night ended, but they both knew tomorrow was going to bring the continuation of their saga.

Jasmine awoke the next morning with the same sick feeling in her stomach. She knew that something was wrong and began preparing herself for the worst. Their conversation ended quickly the night before, but they had issues that still needed resolving. She waited up for him, so she could talk to him about her feelings and the direction of their relationship. As always, he didn't come home when he was supposed to. She began to get concerned. She called his job and his cell phone, no answer. Jasmine called Renee and asked her to come over and go with her to his job. Renee arrived at Jasmine's place within a half an hour.

Renee asked, "What's wrong is everything all right?"

Jasmine responded, "I have a feeling that something isn't right and I need to check it out. Lewis has been acting strange, he has been coming home at odd hours, not answering his work or cell-phone, and we haven't had sex in weeks. I have this feeling in my gut Renee, something is going on. This might sound unusual, but I see him in my dreams being unfaithful. I see him with this woman; she's the same one every time. Do you think I'm being paranoid?"

"Well it's just a dream, don't get worked up over it. Do what you feel you have to do, to give yourself a piece of mind."

"Come on, let's go," Jasmine said with a serious voice.

Renee obliged and said nothing in response. They drove up to his job and to her amazement, his car was in the garage. She looked at Renee and said, "He's here, let's see why Mr. Man hasn't been answering his phones." They walked up to the building and motioned for the security guard to come let them in. He walked over to the door, but wouldn't open it. He pointed to a white intercom on the wall next to the door, instructing them to push the green button.

"Sorry ladies, no one is allowed in the building after working hours. You'll have to come back tomorrow," he said with a husky voice.

"My boyfriend is expecting us. He should have left a message with you," Jasmine yelled back.

"I didn't receive anything for any visitors tonight. I'm sorry I can't let you ladies in," the guard said standing his ground.

Renee thinking, on her feet, came up to the counter and began talking to him. She asked him if he goes out, he replied that he did. They talked a little and he said he recognized her from somewhere. She realized that he was her ex-boyfriend's cousin. He didn't know they were no longer dating. They laughed a little and he told them they could go up. Lewis worked on the 12th floor so the elevator ride seemed endless. Jasmine's heart began to pound harder as the numbers beeped with the passing of each floor.

She looked over at Renee and said, "I hope I'm wrong. Maybe we'll find him asleep at his desk or busy doing work."

Renee looked over giving her a little smile, shaking her head up and down. Renee too had a gut feeling that something was wrong and that Jasmine was in for a surprise. She was just glad to be there to help her in case her fears became a reality. After all Jasmine was her best friend.

Renee had a little secret that she held in from Jasmine. She heard Lewis was seeing someone, but she wasn't going to say anything to her. She knew that in time it would all reveal itself.

The elevator finally reached the 12th floor and they got off. Lewis's office was down the hall, so he couldn't hear the elevator doors open. They walked to the entrance of his office. Taking a deep breath she opened the door. She stood in the doorway and the sight she saw made her speechless. Renee made her way around Jasmine and couldn't believe what she was seeing. If they didn't see it with their own eyes, they wouldn't have believed it. Lewis was having sex in his office. They were going at it so hard, that Jasmine and Renee standing there was at a distant second to their activity.

Lewis had her on the chair, doing her doggy style. Her face was buried in the seat of the chair; his head moved back and forth, like a bobbled head doll. Jasmine's eyes turned crimson from the rage that was building in her. She stared so hard that the sweat rolling off his back looked like red juice drops. She stood there motionless, like a watch with no batteries. Everything around her came to a halt; sounds were silenced to her ear. In an instant, time stood still. "Kill him," flashed in and out of her mind, but she knew that before she arrived, it was over between them. She looked around the room for something to pick-up.

She reflected back on her dreams and now she knows that she wasn't being paranoid. He was busted and all his lies were waiting to be exposed. Renee was trying to hold it in, but it was getting harder. For some reason, she too was feeling some pain from what she was witnessing. Lewis asked a question, and it was the last straw for Jasmine.

He asked, "I want this every night. Can I have it?" She continued moaning, giving no response to Lewis's question.

"Can I have you, all to myself?" he asked.

Jasmine couldn't sit back and watch any longer, she had taken all she could. She walked over to them, hauled back and kicked him between his legs while he was in his full sexual stride. He turned screaming, placing his hands between his legs to protect the area from future contact. The connection sent a wave of pain up through his body. Death at this point seemed like heaven, compared to the feeling he was having. He was in total shock as well as pain, to find

Jasmine staring him down. She stood over him breathing heavily with a gold letter opener clinched tightly in her hand.

"So this is the same ole' same ole' huh? You are worthless. If jail wasn't the outcome of me stabbing you right now, I'd stab you in your heart so you can feel what mine is feeling. Your stuff will be waiting for you outside in the yard. If it's there when I get up in the morning, it's being thrown away. If you knock on my door, I'm calling the police. If you don't believe me, try me." She dropped the opener on the floor and without skipping a beat, kicked him in his ribs. She turned to get Renee when she noticed Renee making gestures to the woman in the chair.

"What's up Renee, you know her?" she asked.

"Yeah! I know the hoe," Renee responded. The woman got up and turned around and to Jasmine's surprise it was her co-worker Natalie. She looked at Jasmine and began to cry.

"I am so sorry, I didn't know he was your man," she said hysterically.

"I should punch you in the face for being a nasty home wrecker. It's not even worth it. You can have his tired ass, By the way if he did this to me, what makes you think he won't do it to you?"

She turned and walked off, but Renee on the other hand was hurting too. She looked at Natalie and without saying a word, slapped her in the face. Natalie fell back in the chair holding her face, crouching in the chair trying to cover her half-naked body. Renee walked passed Lewis, who was still on the floor curled up in pain from the kick Jasmine gave him and kicked him too. She then ran out to catch up with Jasmine.

They got in the elevator and silence filled the air. They walked out, got into the car and drove off. Jasmine's eyes began to fill with tears, she tried to drive but the road began to get blurry. She pulled over, put her head on the steering wheel, and began to cry. Renee tried to comfort her but it did no good. Jasmine felt betrayed. Her love had been destroyed and she felt pieces of her heart leaving her body with every teardrop. She knew from that moment on she could never give her heart to another, in fear of it being broken again. She had given all she had to Lewis and he destroyed it. She could not understand why he would spoil what they had together for a woman half her status. Jasmine had the look, the career, and the sexual appetite to please any man. She is a woman in public and a freak in the bedroom. She sat in her car chatting away.

Renee sat there and did the only thing she knew Jasmine needed at that moment, someone to just listen.

"Where do you know Natalie from?" she asked Renee.

"I've seen her around town, I heard about her. This isn't the first time she had been caught with someone's man."

"I don't need this. I'm through with men. I can do bad all by myself," she added. She finished venting, wiped her eyes and they drove off. They laughed a little about what happened and how funny it was to see their reactions, when Jasmine kicked Lewis in the balls. Jasmine dropped Renee off at her house and headed home. The ride home seemed forever, but she knew it was what she had witnessed that made her drive seem never ending. Jasmine reached her driveway and parked her car. She ran inside threw his belongings in a bag and tossed them on the lawn. She then went in the house and put the dead bolt on, just in case he tried getting in. She took her shower and got into bed trying to fall asleep, but the thought just played repeatedly in her head. Jasmine cried throughout the night and finally drifted off to sleep.

CHAPTER 2

Jasmine took some time off from work to collect her thoughts. She knew that facing Natalie wasn't going to be easy. After all, Lewis was her everything. He was the first for her, the first guy she ever committed to. She hurt more than she wanted anyone to know, even Renee. She finally realized that she was all alone. Her nights were filled with thoughts of him and the things they used to do. No one ever made her feel the way Lewis did and getting over him was going to be difficult. Jasmine arrived at work after a two-week break. She went to her desk and sat there looking at the telephone, wondering if it would ring. If so, would Lewis be on the other end? She was so accustomed to talking to him upon her first arrival to work. She knew that in order to get over him, the last thing she needed was to talk to him. She let the thought pass and began to consume herself in her work. Jasmine had a Bachelors degree in accounting and worked for a plastic surgeon's office as an account manager.

She spent most of the morning catching up on her work. She realized that she hadn't seen Natalie all morning, and really hadn't given it any thought. Just as quickly as the thought came, Natalie showed up. She had been out running errands all morning and didn't realize that Jasmine was back from her vacation. Earlier when Jasmine arrived at work, her assistant Nicole came to welcome her back and catch her up on what had been going on while she was away. She told her of the changes with the company and other things that really didn't interest her. She began telling Jasmine about Natalie and her new man.

"Girl, Natalie has this new man and she has been running around like she has won the lottery, glowing everyday and all chipper. She was telling us about how she loved going home at night, how he loved to have his bath run, and she would have his meal prepared for him," Nicole continued. Jasmine began to feel the hurt, she was trying to get over, resurface.

"She was telling us how she had been up to his job and made passionate love in his office and almost getting caught by the cleaning people," Nicole continued.

Jasmine felt the rage building up inside her and knew that she didn't need to hear any more. Nicole had no idea that Natalie was talking about Lewis. No one else knew of Lewis in the office but Nicole. Jasmine quickly changed the subject and told Nicole that she had to get back to work. She had a lot of catching up to do. Nicole left and Jasmine sat there. Her eyes began to fill with tears, but she knew that it would set her back and she didn't need that.

Lunchtime came and Jasmine decided to go to the cafeteria to get away from her desk. She got her meal and searched for a place to sit, but the place was crowded. She finally found a spot off in the corner, which was perfect for her so she could be by herself. She was enjoying her meal; that was until Natalie and the others came in. They all sat together at a table a short distance away from Jasmine's. Nicole and the other ladies waved, with the exception of Natalie who never even gave her a look. Natalie decided to get back at Jasmine for what she did to Lewis and what Renee did to her. She pulled out some pictures that she and Lewis took at the amusement park last weekend. She made sure that she talked loud enough about their trip so Jasmine could hear. The pictures circled around the table and everyone made comments about how happy they looked together.

One of the ladies turned around and asked, "Jasmine would you like to look at them?" Jasmine smiled and said, "No thanks, you all enjoy them."

Nicole finally received the pictures; she was dying to see them since she had heard so much about him. When she got them she was in complete shock. She turned and looked at Jasmine but quickly turned back around. She didn't want to give them any indication that she knew the guy in the photo. She passed the pictures back to Natalie. Natalie realized that she knew who the guy was and gave her half a smile. Lunchtime was up and they all began to leave. Nicole made her way over to Jasmine.

"I am so sorry about all that back there. I never expected that to be Lewis. I thought you two were happy?" Nicole said. Jasmine told her what had happened, about them being caught together at his office.

Nicole couldn't believe her ears, as she looked at Jasmine in complete shock. "She's a liar. Natalie knew of your relationship with Lewis. I told her who he was when he came to pick you up from work some months ago. I recall Natalie making a comment on how fine he was and how she wanted someone that fine. All this time she has been running around talking about this wonderful guy and how great her life was, how he had changed her life," Nicole grunted out.

Jasmine tried calming Nicole down, but she wasn't getting through to her. "I can't believe this, how could she do that to you?" Nicole continued. "Of all the men in this city, why do woman like that have to prey on already taken men?"

She began to feel Jasmine's pain and felt responsible for it all. She figured that if she hadn't shown Lewis to Natalie they would still be together.

Jasmine told her, "It's okay Nicole, I'm in my healing phase right now. It's not your fault. It was bound to happen with or without Natalie. The hardest part is trying to move on here and having this constant reminder of him and that bitch."

"Come to think about it Jasmine in one of those pictures I saw your girlfriend," she told her.

"What girlfriend?"

"The one you're always with, ummm! What is her name? Regina? No Re…ne," Nicole asked.

"Renee?" Jasmine responded.

"Yeah that's her, I've seen her around here a couple times too. I thought she was here to see you, but I never seen them talk.

"It's probably just a coincidence," Jasmine replied.

"Maybe so," she responded.

"It doesn't matter. I'm contemplating getting another job and moving on with my life. After all, I can get a better job making more than I do here."

Nicole hugged her and responded, "I would understand if you left. I would miss you and for selfish reasons want you to stay."

Nicole left and again Jasmine was left with the thoughts of Lewis and now the thought of Renee possibly being involved in all this. She could hear Natalie's voice in the background. The more she talked the more she was annoyed, wanting so much to go and slap her in the mouth. She knew it wouldn't solve anything.

Jasmine left work; she stopped by the grocery store to get a few things, and ran into Renee. She told her about her day and how bad it was and about her decision to leave. Renee knew this day was going to come, either that or a fight, but she knew Jasmine wasn't the fighting type. She grabbed Jasmine playfully trying to cheer her up and encouraged her to look for another job. She looked at Renee, wanting to ask her about the picture but she knew it wasn't the time or place to do it. Jasmine paid for her groceries and left. Renee ran up to her and handed her the employment section of the paper, smiled and told her everything is going to be alright. Half-smiling back she climbed in her car and drove off. Jasmine arrived home only to be reminded of her past. She decided to rearrange the house and give it a new look. She sat down browsed through the help wanted ads and circled a few options. She got her resume together and planned to send them out first thing in the morning. Her mind was made up to leave. She knew it was the right thing to do, if she wanted to have some peace of mind. She got ready for bed, said a prayer and turned in with hopes that tomorrow would be much better.

CHAPTER 3

Months passed by and Jasmine continued waiting for some type of feedback from the companies she sent her resume. She had a few interviews, but nothing was solid. Things at the office weren't getting any better. Natalie was still being childish and by now everyone knew that Lewis was her ex. She couldn't walk around the office without people expecting the two of them to have a head on collision. If she had a few words with her, she felt the others would think she was being bitter about Natalie and Lewis's relationship.

She knew that something had to happen quickly. She decided to check her email since she hadn't done so all day. There was an email from one of the places she had applied for a job. Nervous about clicking on it, she paused and said a prayer before opening it. It was a request for her to come back for a second interview. She realized that she had a good chance of getting the job. It was another accounting job, but this one was for the local hospital. This job offered more money and better benefits. She was so excited and she called Renee to pass on the good news. She told Renee that the interview was for this coming Thursday and if she got the job they would have to go out and celebrate that weekend.

Thursday arrived and Renee called her first thing in the morning to wish her good luck on her interview. Lewis found out that Jasmine was leaving her job or thinking about leaving, so he called her to wish her luck. Jasmine was shocked to hear from him since she hadn't heard from him in months since the break up and the incident at his office.

"Hey Jazzy," he asked.

Jasmine responding rudely, "What is it, why are you calling me?"

"I just wanted to call and wish you good luck," he said.

"Good luck for what?" she asked.

"On your interview," he replied.

"Thanks. Now what do you really want? You have a few seconds before I hang the phone up."

"I wanted to say I'm sorry for what happened," he softly responded.

Jasmine in a now serious tone, "You're right you are sorry, now understand this: I will never forgive you for the damage you've done to me. You have some nerve calling, oh! I'm sorry and just like that, automatic forgiveness. Hell no! I have suffered for months, trying to get over nightmares of what you put me through, the embarrassment at work and all the constant reminders of the pain from that slut at work. Now that I'm trying to move on, you want to call me and act like you're really concerned," she angrily responded.

"Jasmine you at least owe me..." Before he could finish his sentence, Jasmine said, "Lewis this is what I owe you." She slammed the phone down and walked off with a smile on her face. She had now confronted the issue that was eating her up inside, the last thing that stood in her path to some form of sanity. She continued getting dressed and headed to her interview. The interview lasted about an hour; she got the job and was satisfied with the package. She got to the car and called Renee to tell her the good news.

"Renee, I got the job. I guess we have a date this weekend?"

"Congratulations! Now it's time to let our hair down. It's been a while since we went out," Renee responded. Jasmine told her about the call she got from Lewis and then discussed where they were going to celebrate.

Jasmine decided to go and treat herself at the mall. She figured that it was a new day, a new start, so she would go purchase some new clothes to wear out. She walked around the mall searching for the right dress, a dress that would hug her every curve and place all the attention on all the right parts. She searched all the major stores but nothing really stood out.

She decided to try one of the smaller stores in the nearby plaza. There were a few stores there and she recalled seeing a small boutique in the far corner. So she drove over and pulled up to the window. Jasmine feasted her eyes on the perfect outfit for her night out. The ensemble consisted of a knee length suede skirt and checkered halter-top. She parked and hurried into the store and she tried it on and. It fit perfectly. The outfit even had matching boots. Jasmine knew that she was going to step out and let her hair down with this new look and finally have some fun. Most of all, it was time to see if she could really get on with her life. She purchased the outfit and left the store.

She noticed a tattoo parlor a few stores down. She went to her car and sat there contemplating on getting one. The one she gets will have to symbolize a new beginning. Pondering her choice of tattoo, she just couldn't come up with the right one. After about a half-hour, she came up with the perfect one and the perfect spot to put it. Off to the parlor she went, excited about getting her first tattoo. She was greeted by a very cheerful receptionist when she entered.

"Welcome, how may we assist you today?" the receptionist asked.

"I would like to get a tattoo," Jasmine responded.

"Is this your first?"

"Yes it is," Jasmine said with a nervous smile.

The receptionist asked Jasmine to have a seat so she could explain the policies, procedures, and what she would be required to sign. Carefully reading over everything Jasmine signed the paper work. Now she was ready for her tattoo. John, the tattoo artist, came out and introduced himself to her. Jasmine was getting nervous and John recognized it, "It's alright to be nervous," he said trying to comfort her. "Where would you like it?" he asked.

"I would like it on the small of my back."

John replied, "That's a very sexy spot to put one. I like to call it the genie spot."

"Why do you call it that?" Jasmine asked.

"Rubbed the right way you can make a lot of things come to life, that's a submissive position allowing the man to have control," he laughed.

They laughed a bit and Jasmine said she was ready to get it finished. John told her that he would keep her comfortable and not worry. Jasmine was feeling relaxed after talking with John. She knew she had chosen the right place. John went to work and at first Jasmine was in pain, but after a while she got used to it and lay there thinking of other things. John was just talking and talking about his girlfriend and everything else. It was going in one ear and out the other. Jasmine wondered how many times he told these stories, laughing to herself. It had been almost an hour and Jasmine was getting restless. She wanted to take a break. John agreed and she got up. He showed it to her and she was so excited about the way it was coming out. She was anxious to get it over so she could see the finished product. The break was over and it was time to get back to work.

"Another half-hour and we should be finished," John said. Time was going by so slowly Jasmine thought, but she knew he needed to take his time. She could only think about what Renee was going to say. Renee had been trying to get her to loosen up. "I'm quite sure she wasn't going to expect this," Jasmine thought to herself. John sat up and told Jasmine that he was finished and she can now see the finished product. She went to the mirror. John held the front mirror so that she could get a good look. Jasmine smiled and thanked John for doing a good job. She tipped him well and left with a smile on her face. She got in the car sat for a minute staring at the parlor. A smile came on her face thinking about the comment John made about the spot where she got the tattoo.

Still smiling as she drove off, she looked at the time and didn't realize how late it had gotten. She called Renee and began telling her about her day. Renee was very anxious to see the tattoo. She couldn't believe that she went without her to get it done. That didn't matter, she was very happy for her. They finalized their plans for the evening and then hung up. Jasmine arrived home and laid her outfit on the bed. She then read over the instructions on maintaining her tattoo. It was time for her to shower and get ready to go out. And she had to do something with her hair. She wanted to have a flawless night; she wanted all eyes on her. She still had no interest in meeting anyone. She just wanted to have fun, be wild and live. Although Jasmine longed for love, she just wasn't ready to give it in return. She poured a glass of wine as she got ready, something to calm her nerves.

Renee called, "Are you ready? I'm on my way I should be there in ten minutes," she said.

"I'm ready," Jasmine replied.

She poured another glass of wine and finished it right as Renee knocked on the door. Renee entered screaming, "Let me see it! Let me see the tattoo!" Jasmine pulled her top up and removed the bandage; Renee smiled and told her it was beautiful.

"What made you get that?" she asked.

"I wanted something to symbolize my new start."

"That tattoo was meant for you. It's perfect." She complimented Jasmine on her outfit and said, "Those guys better watch out. Well let's go, it's time to have some fun."

They double-checked the house to make sure they didn't forget anything, then headed out for the evening.

CHAPTER 4

The night was going well. They ended up at one of the spots they had heard on the radio called "Visions". It was a small but comfortable place. This spot was different from what they had expected; it was very intimate and romantic. It was a cellar club in the heart of the city, a nice sized, mature crowd. They checked their coats and headed for a table. The music fit the atmosphere perfectly. They picked a spot where they could have a look at the floor and the club. The waitress came over and took their order. Renee ordered cognac, as for Jasmine, she preferred wine.

"Jasmine the guys were checking you out," Renee said.

"No! They were checking us out," Jasmine said laughingly.

"This is really nice. I can get used to a place like this," Jasmine said.

Almost an hour had passed and they were feeling a little more relaxed. A nice song came on and Renee was anxious to get on the floor, so she began scanning the floor for a dance partner. A guy walked by and asked if either of them would like to dance. Renee jumped on the offer and headed onto the floor. Jasmine, on the other hand, sat and watched Renee do her thing. She continued sipping on her wine and relaxing to the atmosphere. Many men approached her to dance, but she turned them down. One guy stopped and made himself at home in Renee's chair, trying to pick-up Jasmine.

"Would you like something to drink?" he asked.

"Sure," Jasmine said in return.
The drink came and Jasmine thanked him. He sat and made all kind of comments about how beautiful she was and he noticed her when she walked in the room.

"Are you here alone?" he asked. Jasmine, knowing that he was now beginning to make his move with his tired line, decided to cut him off before he got started. "No! I'm not. My girlfriend is on the floor dancing. Besides if you saw me come in you would have noticed her also," Jasmine responded.

"She'll be back soon and I'm sure she will want her chair back," Jasmine continued. He sat there and continued trying to probe Jasmine for information, but she wasn't budging. She realized that he wasn't going to get the hint and since he had bought her a drink, he must feel like he had the right to sit there as long as he wanted. Jasmine waved the waitress over,

"I would like to buy this gentleman a drink, what would you like?" she asked him.

"I would like a shot of Hennessey, thank you," he said to Jasmine. "No problem," she said.

The drink arrived and he seemed to be getting even more comfortable, so Jasmine knew that now was the time to go ahead and burst his bubble.

"I'm sorry, but I only bought you that drink so that we could be even. I don't want you to think that I was using you," she said.

"I wasn't thinking that," he said.

"Well I appreciate the compliments and the drink, but I'm going to have to ask you to leave now. My friend looks like she's winding down and I'm sure she's going to want her chair back."

"I can pull a chair up if that's okay with you?" he asked.

"No, that's not necessary. It was nice meeting you," she said. Jasmine extended her hand for him to shake and he rudely dismissed it and walked off.

Jasmine giggled to herself as she watched him walk off into the crowd. Renee finally made her way back to the table exhausted from dancing. She was trying to catch her breath so she could introduce the guy she was dancing with to Jasmine.

"Tommy this is my best friend Jasmine. Jasmine this is Tommy."

Jasmine stood up and greeted him, "Nice to meet you." As Tommy reached to shake her hand he scanned her up and down, "Likewise," he responded.

Renee noticed him looking over Jasmine. It rather bothered her, so without making a scene she thanked him for the dance. Tommy walked off and Renee said, "What a jerk."

Jasmine turned with a puzzled look on her face asking, "Why would you say that? I thought you guys had fun together?"

"I was, until he started scanning you like you were prey," Renee said annoyingly.

Jasmine was unsure of how to take it, so she left it alone and changed the subject. "I have been approached by some strange guys," Jasmine commented.

"I saw you sitting here with a nice look-ing gentleman, what happened?" Renee asked.

"Oh! That guy? He was only interested in seeing how far he could get, and besides he had some tired lines. He wasn't my type anyway."

"So what is your type? You could have any man in here if you'd like."

"I want a man who could just take me away from reality, show me how to appre-ciate the smell of an ocean breeze. You know someone that can take me on an epic journey through ecstasy and fantasy, with-out the pressure of sex," Jasmine said as she sunk in her chair.

Renee laughed and told her, "Good Luck, those guys only exist in the movies. And besides that kind of stuff is meant for your fantasy world anyway."

The night was coming to an end. Renee danced a few more times, but Jasmine was content with sitting at the table watching the people move about the club. She was in-trigued with the chase the men and women were giving each other in their quest for the perfect mate. Jasmine smiled as she re-membered a scene from a movie that re-minded her of this atmosphere. It reminded her of the cartoon Dinosaurs, when the little male monkeys were scurrying around, jumping, and leaping from vine to vine and female-to-female trying to entice the one that would be their mate. The lights came on and that was the sign that the club was closing, so she gathered all her stuff and waited for Renee to finish exchanging numbers with her last dance partner, so they could leave. They headed home. Renee feeling exhausted, asked Jasmine to just drop her off at home and she'll pick her car up tomorrow. She drove Renee home, sat in the car, and watched to make sure she entered her apartment safely.

Waving as she drove off, she yelled out the car to her, "Call me when you get up!" Renee waved back sluggishly, walked through her door, and closed it behind her. She looked at the time. It was a little after 1 am, and she was feeling restless. Jasmine sat there contemplating whether she should go home or go to the twenty-four hour local café not too far from her place. She decided to go with her first instinct, which was to go to the café and get her favorite muffin and cappuccino. She gave a last glance at Renee's place then drove off, thinking about the night she had and how much fun it was to go out and relax. She turned up the music and began singing as she pulled out of the apartment complex. She rolled down the windows to feel the cool evening breeze on her face.

She let her convertible top down so she could see the sky, "It is such a beautiful night," she said to herself. She started reminiscing about the times she used to sit on the patio deck at night. She used to wonder if there was anyone else looking up at the stars the same time she was. If so were they searching for the same thing she was? Jasmine's mind began to wonder into thoughts of her desires to be swept off her feet. She could feel it in her bones that it could happen despite what others had said, especially Renee. Marvin Gaye came on the radio and Jasmine screamed, "That's my song!" Turning up the volume, she began to sing at the top of her lungs, "Let's get it on!" She forgot about the stars and the fantasy and gave her undivided attention to Marvin as she drove to the café.

CHAPTER 5

Finally, she arrived at the café and as she prepared to get out of her car, a tan truck pulled up a few parking spaces from her. She turned to look out of curiosity, when suddenly a tall gentleman stepped out of the car. He was casually dressed wearing a nice sweater and slacks; he closed his door and glanced towards her. She tried hard to shy away, but something wouldn't let her head turn away. Their eyes met and instantly, it seemed like time froze. It froze long enough for their souls to connect in the heavens. Almost like two magnets pulling each other together. He reached down to straighten his sweater, turned and looked up at the sky, shook his head in a left to right manner, then walked into the café. Instantly she felt a quiver in her stomach and her heart began to race. She sat there trying to regain her composure. Jasmine wanted to start up the car and pull off. She didn't want to tempt the feeling she was having, but she was curious as to what may happen. So she pulled the visor down to get her self together, reapplied her lipstick and fixed her hair that had blown loose from the ride over. Taking a deep breath, she got out of the car. Was she was getting worked up for nothing? "What if my mind was playing tricks on me? What if he was already waiting on someone?" she thought to herself. She opened the door, pretending not to notice him sitting at one of the booths.

Jasmine walked by him and tried hard not to look in his direction, but he spoke to her. "Hello, nice addition you have to your shoes," he said. Jasmine looked down unsure of what he was talking about and there was a piece of tissue stuck to her boots. She looked up at him and they both laughed, as she pulled the tissue off. "Are you here with someone?" he asked.

"No, I'm not."

"It would be my honor if you'd share this big table with me, no need in us sitting alone," he said.

"Sure!" Jasmine said as she removed her jacket. They ordered cappuccinos and muffins and began joking about the tissue and making small talk, both trying to feel the other out.

"What brings a pretty woman out this time of night all alone?"

"It's a long story," she said.

"It normally is," he responded. He extended his hand introducing himself, "My name is Anthony, nice to meet you," he said.

"I'm Jasmine. Nice to meet you too," she said as she shook his hand. "What brings you out?" Jasmine asked.

"I was just stopping in to get a cappuccino and a muffin before I go star gazing."

"Star gazing?" Jasmine said puzzled by his response.

"Yes, I enjoy the stars. Did you know that you and your soul mate share the same star? Have you ever stared at the stars?" he asked.

"Yes!" Jasmine said with a stunned expression on her face. She couldn't believe what she was hearing; her heart began beating uncontrollably again.

He looked into Jasmine's eyes and said, "Sometimes I stare at the stars and wonder if she is staring at them too and if we are staring at the same star." Jasmine bit into her muffin, to keep from making any expressions that may give her away. He continued, "When I'm lonely or going through something stressful I look up at the stars and it always seems to calm me. It's almost as if my soul mate is calming my soul. I know that may sound strange and rather corny."

Jasmine nodded her head no, as she tried to swallow the muffin. While she chewed he continued about the stars. "You may find this strange, but tonight when I was sitting in my car listening to one of my favorite songs on the radio."

Jasmine looked up and prayed he didn't say Marvin. "I was looking up at the stars and I felt a strong connection. It was weird," he said.

Jasmine finished chewing and asked, "What song was it?"

"It was Marvin Gaye's "Let's Get It On," he responded.

Jasmine looked at him trying again not to let her reactions show what she was thinking "That's a nice song. Excuse me I have to go to the ladies room I'll be right back," she said. Jasmine made her way down the hall, trying to maintain her composure. She stormed into the lady's room and paced around, not believing what she had just heard.

"There was no way we could have that much in common, it's a coincidence," she said to herself. Jasmine just could not shake the feeling she was having; she has never felt like this. She thought back to the time she met Lewis and couldn't recall ever feeling like this. All the stories she had heard about the feelings you get when it's love at first sight, she now believed. All the times she dreamt about a fantasy man, could this be that moment where her dreams began to come true? If this is so, how long will this dream last before she had to wake up? She pinched her arm just to make sure she wasn't dreaming, looked herself over one more time and headed out of the bathroom. She decided to let the night take its course, intrigued so far by the conversation. She anxiously headed back out to see what else was going to happen. Making her way back to the table, she smiled at Anthony and then sat down.

"You're very interesting," Jasmine said.

"Why is that?"

"I have never met a man who would open up his sensitive side and share such intimate details about himself, especially to a stranger," she said.

"Well under normal circumstances I wouldn't share that information with someone, then again I don't find this situation normal for me," he responded as he looked into her eyes.

"To be truthful Anthony you and I have so many things in common, like the stars for instance. I love looking at the stars especially when the skies are clear. They're very relaxing," she said. Now sitting comfortably in the booth, still sipping away at her cappuccino, she began to probe him.

"May I ask you a question Anthony?"

"Sure, anything."

"When you got out of your car and glanced at me, you turned and looked up at the stars, and you shook your head. Why was that?"

"It was an unexplainable feeling. My heart began to race, I got goose bumps and kind of dismissed it as being caused by the chill in the air," he replied. Jasmine gazed at him she knew he had felt the same thing she did.

"I hope this will not be too quick for you, but would you like to go star gazing with me?" he asked.

"Now?"

"Yes! Did you forget that's where I was headed before I stopped in here. You can follow me in your car if you would like?"

"I guess I've never been star-gazing, it sounds interesting," she said. Jasmine accepted the invitation, but she said she would follow him. She was feeling spontaneous, but she wasn't a fool. He helped her with her jacket, as she put it on she reached into her pocket to make sure her pepper spray was still there. Jasmine thought, "he seems nice but you never know."

They left the café in separate cars, heading towards the beach. Jasmine couldn't believe that she was actually following through with it. She passed the exit to her apartment and she shortly thought about pulling off. Her heart told her to keep going; besides the beach was only fifteen minutes from where she lived. So far, she liked what she saw in Anthony. He was six feet tall, around two hundred pounds, muscular frame and nice teeth. She fell in love with his childish grin; he had a million-dollar smile. His personality and conversation stimulated Jasmine; he seemed to be a very intriguing man. She knew that if he was anything like what she had seen so far, this could turn out to be more fun than she expected.

They arrived at the beach, finding it vacant. Anthony got out the car first and came over to open Jasmine's door. There was a slight breeze, but it was a romantic chill for a night on the beach. Looking at Anthony, Jasmine asked, "So where do you go to gaze?"

"Hold on," he said as he walked over to his car and popped the trunk. He came back with a blanket and a radio.

"You must do this a lot?" she asked.

"Yes I do! When I come out here I sit on my blanket and listen to my Jazz and relax. You're the first to be here with me. I come here by myself to escape reality and enjoy a little fantasy," he said.

Jasmine was amazed at his comment. That's all she could think about over the past months, was her fantasy world. As they slowly walked down the beach, they came to a spot where the breeze was not too aggressive for them. He began removing any shells, rocks and any debris from the sand before placing the blanket on the ground. He turned on the CD player. Kenny G was playing and his smooth sounds instantly calmed Jasmine's nerves. She leaned back on her arms and held her head back. She was enjoying the breeze and the soothing sound that came from the radio. Anthony placed his head in his hands and took a seat next to her. The breeze was blowing her perfume his way. He inhaled the scent, closed his eyes and absorbed it all in. It was such a lovely smell. He opened his eyes and looked over at Jasmine, who was still in her own world. Starting from her head, he began scanning her. His eyes covered every inch of her body. He was enjoying her peacefulness as she relaxed. Trying not to interrupt her he took one last glance at her and then leaned back, placing his hands under his head. Closing his eyes, he began to visualize Jasmine in his mind. She opened her eyes for the fear of falling asleep. She looked over at Anthony and began to look him up and down, she was feeling nervous.

"What if he opens his eyes and catches me staring at him?" she said to herself. That didn't stop her. She continued looking him over and for every inch she gazed at, it made her insides turn that much more. She longed to be touched; it had been over six months since someone last held her. Her mind began to drift away and she wanted so much for this stranger to open his eyes and take her right there on the beach. She wanted to feel his arms wrapped around her and squeeze her gently. She felt her blood boiling inside and she knew she had to do something to change those thoughts.

"What time is it?" she asked.

"It's almost three in the morning, are you ready to go?" he asked.

"No. I was just wondering, It's getting kind of chilly that's all," she said.

"Hold on. I'll be right back," he said as he got up and ran towards the car. He came back with a fleece sweat suit. "Here you go. You can slip this on, it should keep you warm," he said as he handed her the outfit.

"I couldn't," she said.

"It's ok. I would love for you to put it on. So when I wear it I can have your scent to remind me of you," he said.

Jasmine smiled as she took the outfit. Anthony walked towards the water, with his back to her giving her some privacy. "You can come back," she yelled to him.

Laughing he said, "It fits you very well."

"It's very comfortable," she said about the too big outfit. He reached into his pocket and pulled out a cassette tape. He put it in the deck then pressed play. Jasmine looked at the radio anticipating what she was going to hear. Let's get it on came out and she looked over at him, "You're wrong for that."

"Can I have this dance?" he asked as he held his hand out.

"Sure," she said as she placed her hands in his. Jasmine was trying to keep some distance from him but she began to sink more and more into his arms, like a log in quick sand. She placed her head on his shoulder and felt her body mold to his. She could feel him getting aroused now, but she didn't want to let go. A sense of security came over her and she began to let her guards down. Jasmine noticed the awkwardness from his arousal and adjusted her body to accommodate the swelling.

"I'm sorry about that, should we stop?" he whispered in her ear.

Jasmine's body shivered from Anthony's breath on her ear, responding almost unconsciously, "No! It's rather flattering."

"I thought things like this only happened in the movies," he said.

"That's what people say," Jasmine responded. The song finally ended and another love song came on. Still in each other arms, Jasmine looked up at him with inviting eyes. They stared into each other's eyes, looking beyond the physical and into each other's soul. Anthony's chest swelled from the deep breath he took. Running his tongue over his lips, he leaned toward her. She braced herself for what she had been anticipating for all night, that first kiss. Jasmine placed her arms around his waist, closed her eyes and waited to feel his lips on hers. He ran his fingers through her hair, leaned in and kissed her on the forehead very gently. Then he whispered in her ear, "You're very special. I feel it in my heart and I want to enjoy this moment the way it is."

Jasmine smiled as he hugged her, "I enjoyed this evening, thanks for everything."

"You're welcome," he responded. He reached down to pick up the blanket and radio and they began walking towards their cars. They exchanged numbers, hugged and said their good-byes. They pulled off heading in separate directions. Jasmine followed him through her rear view mirror until he faded into the darkness. She smiled as she headed towards her place. Jasmine couldn't help but wonder why he didn't try anything. She knew that most men in that situation would have tried something. She thought maybe he had someone already and he was caught up in the moment. She had never felt like this before and couldn't help but wonder if he did make a move would she have stopped him or did she really want him to try. She thought about her principles, morals and most of all how she would have judged herself in the morning. She was feeling vulnerable and the chemistry may have caused her to give in to this stranger. Give him what she had held from men for six months and in one night be willing to let him use her as his private playground. He made her feel like she was taking a tour through heaven.

She reached her apartment and couldn't believe she had stayed out this late, but she had no regrets about it. She put his number on the counter in the kitchen, took a glance at it and smiled. She took her shower and crawled in to bed, looking forward to dreaming about Anthony and their encounter.

CHAPTER 6

Rising with a smile, Jasmine sat up in the bed unsure of what to make of the night she just had. She went into the kitchen to check the counter to see if the number was there and if the evening were real. His number lay there on a crumbled brown piece of paper that was torn off a bag he had in his car, Anthony 524-9891. She sniffed and smelled the fragrance of a man's cologne; she smiled as she picked up the paper. He had sprinkled some of his cologne on it. She put the paper down and it fell over to the backside. She glanced down and saw some writing on the back. She picked it up and it read, *JUST A LITTLE REMINDER OF ME*. She couldn't recognize the name of it but the smell was soothing to her soul. Jasmine sat on her sofa and closed her eyes. As she smelled the paper she felt a rush go through her body. She began to reminisce about her night with Anthony and how the wind had blown his cologne right pass her nose, causing her insides to tingle. She could vision him lying on the blanket the outline of his body next to hers. The telephone rang and she looked at it anticipating it to be Anthony calling to say hello.

She picked up the phone with a smile, "Hello," she said with a sexy voice.

A sluggish voice on the other end responded, "Hey Jasmine what's going on, I'll be over later to get my car."

"Oh! It's only you, what's going on Renee?" Jasmine said disappointingly.

"Nice to talk to you too," Renee said back sarcastically.

"Sorry Renee I didn't mean anything by it," Jasmine apologized.

"Were you expecting a call from someone?"

"As a matter of fact I was, I met someone last night."

"I didn't know you met anyone you were interested in from the club," Renee said puzzled.

"I didn't meet him at the club, I met him at the café," Jasmine said in a calm voice.

"Do tell."

Jasmine laid out the whole evening from the time she dropped her off at home to the time she got home.

"Wow! When do you plan on seeing him again?" Renee asked.

"We didn't make a date so I guess I'll have to play it by ear," Jasmine said.

"So Jasmine do you think he's the one for you?"

"This is different. I don't think he's the one, but I do know there's something different about him." Jasmine continued as she sank into her sofa, "Renee the way he looked at me, he looked into my eyes but I felt him staring into my soul. When we danced on the beach, I could feel his heart beating against my chest. I felt like I've known him for years. I felt so safe and secure. I had no worries."

Renee laid back on her bed listening contently to Jasmine as she described her encounter even deeper than before.

"I hope I'm not boring you with this?" Jasmine asked.

"No girl continue, I'm enjoying this, it sounds like something out of a movie or one of those romance novels," she said.

"I just have to tell you this stuff or I'll explode," Jasmine said with a little laughter in her voice. "Renee he was such a gentleman he didn't try anything and girl the way I was tingling inside he could have done just about anything he wanted to me last night. I have never had that happen to me and I tried so hard to control myself, but I just couldn't. My feelings, hormones, and emotions were on autopilot. As we danced it seemed like the world had stopped and everyone and everything was watching us," Jasmine continued as if she was experiencing a high school crush.

Jasmine and Renee carried on the conversations about the evening when Jasmine's phone beeped, "Hold on Renee let me get this, it maybe him."

"Hello!" Jasmine said with excitement in her voice. Again disappointed by the voice on the other line, "What do you want Lewis, why are you calling me?" responding with anger in her voice.

"I know that it's been a while, but I was just calling to see how you were doing. You've been on my mind a lot and I was wondering if we could get together and talk?" he asked.

She took the telephone away from her face and stared at it in shock, from the statement he just made. "How dare you call to ask me a stupid question like that? What makes you think I want to sit and talk to you? First, I would appreciate it if you didn't call here again. Secondly, I have moved on with my life and I suggest that you do the same," Jasmine responded with anger.

"I want you back Jasmine, I know what I did was wrong and I am willing to do whatever it takes to make it up to you."

"You know Lewis you sound like a record skipping on the same beat, playing the same old song. A man makes a mistake with a good woman, now he's sorry and begs for her back. Let me be honest with you, Lewis I only wanted you to love me unconditionally just as I loved you. I did all I could to make you happy I gave you all of me and more," Jasmine responded in a stern voice, as she continued. "I'm glad you called me because I have been wanting to get some things off my chest and there is no better time than the now to do it. So you want to talk, let's talk better yet let me start. Oh! I forgot I have someone on the other line, hold on a second, I will be right back."

She had forgotten that she had put Renee on hold she clicked over "Renee you still there."

"Yes I'm still here. I thought you had forgotten about me. Who was that?"

"You'd never guess!"

"Anthony," Renee probed.

"No, it's Lewis and I think it's time I let him know what I think and how I feel about him. I'll call you when I'm finished okay?"

"Okay, but call me on my cell," she responded with concern and hung up.

She clicked back over to Lewis hoping he was still on the phone. "You still there?" she asked.

"Yes, I'm here who was that, your new man?" Lewis asked.

Jasmine laughed, ignoring the question she continued where she had left off. "Lewis, I trusted you with my heart, mind, body and soul and you abused it. I sat and wondered where did I go wrong, did I run you into her arms, was I not giving you something?" Jasmine said as her eyes began to fill. "Every night I laid in my bed afraid of seeing the visions of you and Natalie in your office. All I could think of is how could you do this to me, I thought that I had it all and you showed me that the only thing I had was my fantasy. I would have loved you forever," Jasmine said as tears began to roll down her cheeks.

"I am so sorry for hurting you Jazzy, I care so much about you. Can we please work this out?" he asked with concern in his voice.

"Lewis I was in love with you, I loved you with all I had to give, I would have given you the world if I could. I made love to you when you wanted it even if I wasn't up to it. I cooked for you, washed your clothes and helped pay your bills. I know that you were there for me at times and I thank you. When did you realize that you missed me, was it the nights you spent in your apartment, all alone? Was it the nights you and Natalie didn't get along or was it right after the sex when you realized that you and her really didn't have anything in common?" Jasmine said with a serious tone in her voice and her eyes still filled with tears.

"Answer me Lewis!," she said demandingly. "You want to talk? Lets talk about how you gave up all we had for a piece of ass, was she worth it? My soul has a hole in it and it burns every time the wind blows, that's how bad you hurt me," she said trying so hard not to break down on the telephone.

Lewis tried to respond but Jasmine was leaving him no room to respond. She was using this time to get everything out in the open. "You hurt me Lewis, your unfaithfulness showed just how much I meant to you, how much our relationship meant to you. It was all a lie and I could never trust you as long as I live. I hope that life's journey treats you well and that God forgives you, because I won't," she responded as her tears begin to take over her face. Lewis finally got a few words in as Jasmine wiped her face.

"I am sorry that I hurt you, how can I make it up to you?" he asked. Jasmine just sat there with the telephone on her cheek not saying a word.

Lewis continued, "Natalie and I are no longer together I left her, because I wanted you back and I know we can work it out. Just give me another chance, I promise things can go back to the way it used to be."

Jasmine was still in her silent mode, searching for the words to say to him.

"Please say something my life is incomplete without you, say you'll give me another chance," Lewis said as tears fell from his eyes.

Jasmine opened her eyes, collected herself and in a soft voice said, "Your best bet is to call Natalie and beg her to take you back. Save those tears for someone who cares. You're nothing but a liar, a cheater and a heartbreaker and I don't ever want to see your face or hear your voice again. This time Lewis this goodbye is forever," she said as she slammed the phone down. Jasmine sat up and leaned forward placing her head in her hands, trying hard to fight back the tears. Unable to stop the tears she just let go and they begin to fall like a wild river. Painfully saying in a loud voice, "Why me Lord, what did I do to deserve this hurt," as her eyes turned blood shot red and her nose started to run, sniffling to stop the fluids from falling.

She grabbed some tissue to clear her nostrils and some water for her dry throat. Sitting there with the thoughts of Lewis and the pain, he caused her. Jasmine thought she had gotten over the hurt, but hearing his voice just brought back so many hurtful memories. Jasmine laid back on the bed and stared up at the ceiling, wishing she could forget the pain and go on with her life. Trying so hard to think of something else besides Lewis, she began to reminisce about her wonderful night.

CHAPTER 7

Monday came along with the start of a new workweek. Jasmine awakes with a smile on her face. She smiled from the thought of her wonderful weekend, especially her encounter with Anthony. Jasmine got herself together for work wondering if she would hear from him again, since she hadn't heard from him since their encounter. She began to walk out the door when her telephone rung; she turned and figured it to only be Renee ignoring the telephone she turned and closed the door behind her. Jasmine got in her car and for the strangest reason, but she couldn't stop thinking of Anthony. She took her disc of Marvin Gaye and stuck it in the deck of course putting it on her favorite song. She pulled off singing right along with him. She pulled his number out as she had done many times, contemplating on using it. Being a little old fashion girl, she put it away waiting for him to make the first move.

Her cell-phone rung, she turned her song down and answered, "Hello."

"Hey girl what's going on, how was the rest of your weekend?"

"What's up Renee it was okay, I didn't do much just hung out around the house."

"So I take it you haven't seen your friend lately?" Renee asked being nosey.

"No I haven't I wonder if he was really into me or was it just one of those moments that happened and you move on," Jasmine responded with disappointment in her voice.

"I'm sure that's not the case, well I have to go I was just being nosey since you don't have anything juicy to tell me, I'll talk to you later. Maybe we'll do lunch I'll call you," Renee said as she hung up. Jasmine laughed, turned up the radio and headed to work. Today was the first day on her new job so she planned to have a long hectic day. She hoped that she would like her new position and would make a good first impression.

Finally arriving at work, she took a deep breath and headed inside. She was greeted by the receptionist.

"Welcome, may I help you?" she asked.

"Yes! I'm new here and I'm not sure where my work area is located, by the way is Mrs. Sanchez in?" Jasmine inquired.

"Sure one moment I'll get her for you and your name is?" the receptionist asked.

"Jasmine," she responded.

"She'll be right out, my name is Erin nice to meet you," she said as she extended her hand for Jasmine to shake.

"Nice to meet you too," Jasmine responded as she returned the handshake. Mrs. Sanchez came out to take her to her work area and give her a brief run down on what she expected from her and what she can expect from the company. They talked for about an hour before Jasmine was left alone in her area. She called Renee to give her the work number and her schedule for the week.

"Is lunch still on?" Jasmine asked.

"Sure the usual spot," Renee responded.

"Sure," Jasmine agreed.

Lunch came quickly and she headed out the door to go meet up with Renee. Arriving at their typical lunch spot, as usual Renee had the table reserved for them. Jasmine sat there alone waiting on Renee, she stared out the window watching the people as they scurried about. She looked at the couples in particular. She started to daydream about Anthony and wonder what he's doing; it was driving her crazy that he had not called her yet. Renee walked up causing the thoughts of him to disappear.

"You must be thinking about something deep, you didn't even notice me walking up," Renee said with a laugh.

"Oh! It wasn't nothing I was just thinking about work," Jasmine responded with guilt in her voice.

"So how's the first day on the new job?" Renee asked.

"It's going fine, I didn't realize that it would be so much work," she said. The waitress came over and took their order. Renee ordered potato skins and Jasmine ordered a Caesar salad. The waitress returned fifteen minutes later with their meals and drinks. Renee began to prepare her meal; Jasmine looked up at Renee and just watched her as she placed everything in their respective place. She placed her drink to the side, the fork to one side of the plate and the knife to the other. She placed the napkin on her lap and seasoned her meal. Jasmine had a feeling in her spirit that was over whelming and without hesitation, reached out her hands across the table and asked Renee to hold her hands. Renee shockingly looked up at Jasmine, to see her facial expression to be a very serious one.

"Are you okay Jasmine, what's wrong?" Renee asked.

"I was just looking at you and just wanted to thank you for being a true friend and always being there for me," Jasmine said.

"Jasmine, that's what friends are for," Renee responded.

"I wanted to do something, for the first time I would like to say a prayer together for our friendship," Jasmine said.

"You're not getting all religious on me are you?" Renee responded with a puzzled look on her face.

"No! I just felt an urge to do it, so just give me your hands," Jasmine said as she gestured for Renee to put her hands in hers. Jasmine began to pray:

"Dear God thank you for allowing us to wake one more day, thank you for our life, health and strength. Thank you for our friendship and the special bond that we share. I pray that you allow no one or material things to come between our friendship." As Jasmine prayed, Renee opened her eyes to look at her, as Jasmine continued praying Renee looked at her and realized that she had become and was becoming a different person. She was no longer the heart broken, needy and lonely person she once knew. She slowly closed her eyes and put her head down, so Jasmine wouldn't realize that she was looking at her. Jasmine was ending her prayer.

"And I ask that you bless the meal before us, in your name we pray amen."

"Amen," Renee also concluded.

"Okay lets eat then," Jasmine said with a smile.

Well into their meal, there was complete silence; it was almost a change in the atmosphere. For the first time, they had nothing to discuss. Renee finally broke the silence. "So! Have you spoken with Anthony yet?" she said with an inquiring tone in her voice.

"No, not yet he must be busy, he'll call when he's ready," Jasmine responded.

"Why don't you call him, maybe something went wrong, maybe he lost your number," Renee continued to push.

"Here you can use my phone," Renee suggested as she reached for her telephone.

"No! That's okay I just want to enjoy lunch right now, maybe I'll call him tonight," Jasmine said as she declined her offer. Besides Jasmine knew that if she used her telephone, his number would be in there and she didn't want her calling him being nosey and messing up anything. They finished their lunch and prepared to head back to work. They hugged and went their separate ways. Jasmine arrived back at work; Erin the receptionist greeted her.

"Well aren't we the lucky one today?" she remarked with a big grin on her face. Jasmine unsure of what she was talking about, looked at her with a puzzled grin.

"Why am I so lucky?" Jasmine responded.

"You'll see it's on your desk," Erin remarked still smiling, leaving Jasmine with no clue about her surprise.

Jasmine made her way to her work area, only to be greeted by a dozen yellow roses. They were as bright as the morning sun. With the biggest grin on her face, she leaned over to take in the sensual aroma that consumed the air. She reached over to retrieve the card attached to it. Unsure of who could have sent the flowers, she hesitantly opened the card. It was a congratulation card wishing her luck on her first day at her new job. She turned to read the inside of the card; there she saw a poem written in red ink. "Untitled, what a name," she said with a smile as she began to read.

UNTITLED

A chill through my spine running wild
Thoughts of you kept my soul in exile
Visions of your lovely face dancing in my
mind
Dreams of you and I cannot be declined
Fragrance of you still lingering in the air
More of that night I hope we can share
Destiny is strange with stories left untold
I'm curious as to see how this will all un-
fold
I thought of you often but didn't know
what to say
So I talked to the stars hoping they
would guide you my way
I still feel the rush, from your sensual
touch
Never realizing I would miss it that much
I hope you like your gift and I hope to see
you someday
Smile and I hope that this has brighten
your day

Jasmine placed her head in her hands
and tears began to flow, she had never received flowers at work before. The poem
was so sweet and it was even more special,

because he actually wrote it. She was so overwhelmed that she picked up her telephone to call him and thank him for the gifts. She waited for him to pick up, but only the voice mail came on.

"Hello! This is Jasmine, I received your surprise and I really enjoyed it, I hope to hear from you soon." She hung up and sat back in her chair basking in her glory, as she stared at the flowers and the thought of how considerate he was for doing what he did. She wished that she could talk to him and personally thank him, but she couldn't get a hold of him.

"Jasmine!" A voice echoed through her area, bringing her back to reality. It was Mrs. Sanchez summoning her to follow in stride as she turned and walked off. Jasmine obliged, took another glance at her flowers then turned and followed her supervisor down the hallway.

CHAPTER 8

Arriving at home, Jasmine kicked off her shoes, headed towards her room and prepared for her usual shower, feeling a need to relax. She decided to take a candlelight bubble bath instead, pour some wine and listen to some jazz. Tonight was going to conclude her wonderful day. She began prepping her water, wine and candles. The volume on the stereo was perfect, and she was now ready to slip into the tub. She turned to get the card that Anthony wrote her. She wanted to read those beautiful words until she had them memorized. She settled in the water, opened the card and began reading. She began to reminisce about the night they met. How he had aroused something inside her that made her want to know more about him. She realized that he had her curiosity peaked. She finished reading the card and placed it back in the envelope. She noticed some writing on the back of the card CALL TONIGHT 323-2210. Thoughts began running through her mind.

"Is this another number for him?" she thought as a smile came over her face. She reached to pick up the phone, paused and began dialing the number. There was no answer, she figured it was a wrong number or she had called too late. She went to hang up the phone when she heard someone talking.

"Hello! Welcome to Fantasy Massage the ultimate getaway, where it is our job to take you away from reality. If you are calling for the Hawaii package press one. If you are calling for the European package press two. If you are calling for the Far East package press three or stay on the line for your fantasy operator." Jasmine was unsure of where she was calling, but she stayed on the line curious as to what this was all about. A few minutes passed by before the operator came on.

"Hello! My name is Marie and I will be your fantasy guide, how may I help your fantasy getaway come to life?" she asked.

"Well I am really unsure of why I'm calling you, I was given this number with a gift," Jasmine responded.

"May I have your last name please?" asked the operator.

"Simmons," she replied.

Jasmine sat in the tub with great curiosity she had no clue as to what was going on, but the suspense was driving her crazy.

"Yes, Ms. Simmons you are scheduled for the Hawaii Platinum Package, when would you like to schedule your getaway?" she asked.

"I'm still unsure of what you're talking about, can you fill me in on this Hawaii package?" Jasmine asked

"Well it seems that someone took great measures to ensure that you had the best package we could offer. It consists of a limousine ride to the getaway and back to your residence. I'm sorry Ms. Simmons but there are instructions here to not give you any further information," she replied.

"So what am I suppose to do from here?" she asked.

"The message says for you to pick a Saturday and set aside that evening for your getaway and don't worry, all of your expenses have already been taken care of. Which Saturday this month would you like? There's an opening for this coming Saturday should I pencil you in?" she asked.

"Sure I guess I'm feeling adventurous, let's go with this coming Saturday," Jasmine responded.

"Okay Ms. Simmons I will schedule you for Saturday the 12th at 5pm, you will be picked up at what location?" she asked.

"You can pick me up at 51 Sanders Street," Jasmine responded.

"The limo will be there a quarter to five, I must say you are in for a royal treatment. Are there any questions before I let you go?" she asked.

"No! I'm okay for now if I do have any I will call," she responded.

"Enjoy your day and I look forward to meeting you, goodbye," she said as she hung up the phone.

Jasmine sat there staring at the ceiling, wondering what just happened and what was about to happen. She was very curious about this massage place and had to share this with someone so she decided to give Renee a call. She called her, hoping that she was home. Her answering machine picked up.

"You have reached Renee sorry I can't come to the phone right now, but if you leave your name and number I'll get back with you as soon as I can."

Jasmine spoke into the answering machine, "I need you to call me as soon as..."

"What's going on?" Renee said as she picked up the telephone interrupting Jasmine's message. Jasmine anxiously told her about the flowers, card and the gift certificate.

"Have you ever heard of this place called Fantasy Massage-the ultimate getaway," Jasmine asked.

"Yes! I've I heard of it, it's one of the most talked about spots in town. One of the girls I work with went there her and her husband," Renee commented.

"Did they like it?" Jasmine asked.

"Yes! She said it was unlike anything she had ever seen, she said they had the Basic European Package," Renee said.

"Well, the gift certificate is for the Hawaiian Platinum Package, the operator said it was the best package they had," Jasmine said.

"Wow! He must really be into you, because I heard it was costly to go there. It must be nice to have it like that," Renee continued.

"I don't have it any kind of way, what are you talking about?" Jasmine said defensively.

"I'm just saying you've only known this guy for a few days and only met him once and he's already spending this kind of money on you," Renee said sarcastically.

"Well I can't control how he thinks, I think it's sweet and thoughtful," Jasmine responded.

"Well I'm just saying be careful you never know these days about people, especially someone whom you met in a café, at God knows what time in the morning," Renee remarked.

"I am not going to let you ruin my mood, so I'll call you later okay," Jasmine said.

"Okay!" Renee said as she hung up the phone.

Jasmine looked at the telephone in amazement; she couldn't believe what just took place. She was starting to wonder if Renee was getting jealous. Dismissing the thought of that happening, she couldn't imagine her best friend being envious about her happiness. With all the conversations that took place, Jasmine realized that her water was no longer warm and the bubbles had disappeared. The relaxing atmosphere she had been looking forward to enjoying didn't go the way she had planned. Renee had ruined her mood and all she wanted to do was lay down and get some rest. She got out of the tub dried off, prepared to lie down, turned on the television and climbed into bed. Lying in the bed, she began having thoughts about Anthony. She contemplated on whether or not to call him. For a few seconds, she stared at her telephone before deciding to try him again. The phone ranged four times before his voice mail picked up. The message was a generic recording, so hearing his voice was out of the question. She hung up in disappointment, rolled over and turned the television off.

She kneeled on the floor and began her evening prayer. This had been her ritual ever since she was a little girl. Finishing her prayer she climbed back into bed and stared at the flowers sitting on the dresser. Wondering what Anthony was doing, why he wasn't returning her calls and why he was doing all these wonderful things for her. She wasn't complaining, since he wasn't doing her any harm. He was just a nice and considerate man; she just wanted to spend more time with him. Over all she had a good day and wasn't going to let Renee ruin her moment.

She laid down on her queen sized, cherry wood, sleigh bed, looked up to heavens, closed her eyes, smiled and said, "Thank you God for another day."

CHAPTER 9

Jasmine sat at her desk, wanting so bad to ask Renee about her connection with Natalie and her potential jealousy. She decided to call her about what was happening and see if she was okay. She called her at work. While waiting for her to pick up; she started getting her thoughts together hoping to not offend her.

"Stanley's Mortgage, Renee speaking. How may I direct your call?"

"Hello! Renee it's me Jasmine."

"What's going on?" Renee asked.

"I was just calling to see if you were okay, last night we got off the phone rather strange," Jasmine responded.

"I'm okay, I was just being concerned that's all," Renee said.

"Okay so everything is cool?" Jasmine asked.

"Everything is cool," Renee said in a sly voice.

"By the way Jasmine have you heard from Lewis?" she asked

"No! I haven't why are you asking me about him?" Jasmine asked with a concerned voice.

"Just wondering, he called the other day asking how you're doing and if I still hung out with you. You know he still cares about you and feels really bad about what he did," Renee said.

"I have nothing to say to him, I have moved on with my life and from my eye sight he is no longer in the picture, so I suggest that he does the same. I know you two are still cool, but I would appreciate it if you kept his messages to yourself please," Jasmine said in a serious tone.

"I was just checking, well you know he's a good man and they do make mistakes," Renee said in Lewis' defense.

"Well he made one mistake too many. Answer this for me, how do you get over catching your man having sex with another woman? If you can tell me how to get over that, I would like that information very much. You know Renee lets just change the subject, are we still on for lunch?" Jasmine asked.

"I can't make it today I have other plans, but lets meet up tomorrow," Renee responded.

"Okay!" Jasmine said as she sat in her chair again puzzled by Renee's response.

"I'll call you later, I have to get this other line. Bye now," Renee said as she hung up.

Jasmine sat back and wondered what was going on with Renee, first last night and now today. This is the first time Renee missed lunch, even during the snowstorm they would get together. Not letting Renee get to her, she picked up the phone and called Anthony, just like all the other times his answering service came on. She hung up in frustration, refusing to leave a message.

Jasmine's phone rang. She picked it up, "Jasmine speaking how may I help you?"

"Hello Jasmine it's me Lewis, how are you doing?" he asked.

"Just the person I didn't want to hear from. I'm fine and how did you get this number? Oh! Never mind I know where you got it from," Jasmine said in an angry tone.

"I told you I didn't want to hear from you, so why are you calling me?" she continued with her tone escalating.

"I just wanted to say hello and see how you were doing, but I can still hear the hatred you have for me in your voice," he said.

"I asked you to back up and leave me alone, but you just don't get it do you? I hate you and I don't want to hear your voice or see your face ever again, so please, please leave me alone," she said as tears began to fall from her eyes.

"I still love you Jasmine and I would do anything to have you back in my life, give me one more chance," he said in a sincere voice.

"I can't, won't and never will" she said and slammed the phone down. Her tears began to fall increasingly, forgetting that she was at work. Jasmine collected herself wiped her tears and fixed her makeup. She thought about the call and her temper began to boil, she couldn't believe that Renee gave him her number. She picked up the phone and dialed Renee's work number then hung up the phone realizing that talking to her would only make her angrier than what she already was. She sat back in her chair, took a deep breath, and went back to work trying to put Lewis out of her mind. Time flew by and before she knew it, it was almost time to go home.

"Jasmine, there's a package at the desk for you," Erin said speaking through the intercom system. Jasmine went to the front to retrieve her package, making her way to the desk.

"Erin those are some beautiful roses, do you have a package for me?" she said as she dismissed the presence of the roses.

"Yes, this is your package, you must be pretty special to someone?" Erin said gesturing to the dozen red roses.

Jasmine smiled, smelled the roses and carried them back to her desk. Unlike the roses she got before, the feeling that came over her was different. That tingling feeling that she had when she saw the yellow roses was much stronger. Jasmine picked up the note attached to the vase and read it.

Jasmine;

I miss you so much and really want to make things up to you. I think of you all the time, when I close my eyes I only see you. I see your eyes staring into mine; I feel my heart pounding rapidly when I think of you. I made a mistake. You not being here for me and with me is the price I had to pay. I feel like all the oxygen around me is leaving, because it's so hard to breathe without you. I pray that

I will be able to feel your touch again, stare into your eyes as we lay in each other arms. To feel the passion and the fire that once burned. If I have to start all over from scratch, I will start the fire one log at a time. Wow and amazing are the words that come to mind when I think of you. I hope there's something in you, that in the times we've had together something good is still there. I cry at night for you to give me another chance, my soul longs to hear from you. The only thing it gets back is an echo from a lonely heart. Please forgive me, I will be waiting with open arms. I MISS YOU

Lewis

Jasmine couldn't believe that he had sent her some flowers. "Erin can you come here please," Jasmine asked of her over the speaker phone.

"One second Jasmine and I'll be right there," she responded.

"Yes how can I help you?" Erin asked.

"Well I know that you like flowers and I want you to have these, you can sit them out front so everyone can enjoy them," Jasmine told her.

"Sure! May I ask why you're not taking them home?" she inquired.

"Well I already have some at home and besides there a nice gesture from someone I once knew, but I really don't like red roses," Jasmine responded.

Erin obliged picked up the flowers and walked out, puzzled by the comment that Jasmine made. Jasmine took the card, ripped it into little pieces, and tossed it into the trash. It was now time for her to leave work; she picked up her keys and jacket and headed out the door. Jasmine wanted so much to scream, but with the other people on the elevator, she knew that it wouldn't be a good idea.

Finally making it to her car, she hopped in and turned the car on. She placed in her favorite disc, grabbed the steering wheel, put her head down and screamed. She lifted her head up and drove off, wondering why he wouldn't leave her alone. Jasmine called her house to check her messages hoping that there would be a call from Anthony. There were a few messages one from her finance company, someone trying to get her to change her long distance service but no call from Anthony. She pulled out the parking lot and headed down the strip looking at the shops and wondering if she should stop and get something for her evening at the massage parlor. The thought quickly faded when she saw Lewis walking towards Renee's building. She pulled over and watched to see what was going on. Renee came out greeted him with a hug. Jasmine noticed their embrace was a little longer and more affectionate than normal. She sat and watched them laugh and joke then walk off together holding hands. She sat in awe, having just received roses and a card from him.

Although they were no longer together, seeing her best friend and her ex-boyfriend together like that hurt her. She sat there and thought about it but didn't want to jump to conclusions. Contemplating on whether to confront them or not. She fought the tears from coming down and refused to let them mess up her upcoming weekend at the massage parlor. She watched in astonishment as they walked away, until they were no longer in sight. She wiped her eyes of the little tears that were trying to fall and drove off.

Jasmine arrived at home and checked her machine. There was one message from the massage parlor. They were trying to get confirmation for her appointment. After calling them back and confirming the time and date, she sat on her sofa poured a glass of wine and tried not to think about what she saw. It was a difficult task for her because of the picture on top of the end table. A picture of her, Renee and Lewis at the amusement park. Jasmine got up and walked into her bedroom determined not to allow it to get to her. She finished her glass of wine she sat on the bed feeling ripe for the picking and wanted to be picked by Anthony. The more she thought about her day the more she wanted to be taken away into a sexual bliss of passionate lovemaking. Her mind began to fantasize and she knew it was time to be relieved. Her insides were now becoming more active, like a waking volcano. She turned picked up the telephone and called Anthony trying to control her breathing. She didn't want him to hear the lust in her voice.

She anticipated him to answer; as usual, she got the machine, "Hello! Anthony this is Jasmine I was calling to see if you wanted to get together and maybe have a drink and talk. If you get this message call me it doesn't matter about the time, talk to you later,"

Sitting there, she wondered why she hadn't been able to talk to him...that in itself was driving her crazy. She lay there hoping that he would call, but the night passed by and there was no call from him.

CHAPTER 10

Awakened by the ringing of the telephone, Jasmine rolled over wiped her eyes to see what time it was.

"I can't believe this," Jasmine said with a grumpy voice. "It's two o'clock in the morning this had better be good," she shouted. She reached across the night stand to pick-up the telephone.

"Hello!" she said angrily.

"Sorry for waking you up, but I need to talk to you," he said.

"Lewis?" Jasmine asked.

"Yes! I couldn't sleep and I needed to talk to you," he repeated.

"At two in the morning, Lewis what's going on why can't you leave me alone?" Jasmine said as she attempted to wake fully.

"I was sitting here tossing and turning and couldn't sleep, all I keep thinking about is you. I need you Jasmine," he begged.

"Lewis, please go on with your life, I have, all you're doing is hurting yourself and driving me to despise you," she said.

"Can you please forgive me? I need you in my life. Can we try our relationship again?" he asked.

"We have nothing. All I had for you is gone. Yes, I loved you once, I was in love with you, but now all of that is gone," she said.

"I've changed. All I ask is that you give me another chance," he begged in a now tearful voice.

"You're getting worked up Lewis and believe me I hate seeing you like this, but you did this to yourself now you have to deal with it the best way you can," she told him.

"Jasmine, I love…," he tried to say.

The thoughts of what she saw earlier, those words made her sick to her stomach. "Before you finish that sentence I am about to cut you off, I don't want to hear it ever again from you. You can't possibly mean it, the way you have treated me and I am tired of going through this cycle with you so please, go call your new girlfriend. One more thing I am changing my numbers here and at work and I won't be giving them out so don't try and get it from Renee because she won't have it," she said.

"I bet Anthony will get it," he said sarcastically.

"I am not even going to respond to that or even ask how you know about him, on that note good-bye Lewis," she said as she hung up the phone. Jasmine rolled over, grabbed her pillow, and vented her frustration into it. Now calm she realized that she couldn't change the number in case Anthony tried to call. She couldn't believe that he called saying the things he said, when she had just seen him and Renee together.

Lewis sat on his sofa, holding his head, as sweat beads rolled off his forehead from the heat his body had generated from the anger. Thoughts of Jasmine and this guy she was seeing had his mind going insane. The thoughts of them together ran through his head and he couldn't shake it. He got up and began taking shots of rum, the more he thought about it the more he drank. He moved from the shot glass, to turning up the bottle. He sat down on the sofa and pulled out a photo album, reminiscing about the times they shared. Tears began to fall like raindrops; his heart began pounding out of control. It was almost as if it was trying to break through his chest. He began looking around for the phone. He needed someone to talk to; finally, he found it in between the sofa pillows. If anyone could ease his stress, it would be Natalie. He wasn't sure how solid that was, since he hasn't spoken to her in a few weeks. Maybe she could help ease his pain and take his mind off Jasmine.

She picked up the telephone with her voice full of energy, "Hello!" Natalie said.

"Hello! It's me Lewis did I wake you," he asked in his drunken voice.

"Wow! Look what the cat drug in. How are you stranger?" she said in a sarcastic voice.

"I'm doing okay. I was wondering if we could get together, I was thinking about you and wanted to see you," he said pitifully.

"Well, I'm sure that you have been thinking about me and I was thinking about you too," she said.

"Really about what?" he said in an exciting tone.

"I was just wondering, you know sweetie how you treated Jasmine. All you did just to be with me and if I was your girl would I receive the same treatment?" she said in a now serious tone.

"I wouldn't do that to you, I care about you," he said.

"What do you care about? You cared about the sex, Lewis," she said.

"That's not true! I loved our moments together, but that wasn't the only thing I cared about," he stated.

"What did you want from me then? Why did you mess with me if you had someone?" she asked.

"You caught my attention and after talking to you, I was interested in knowing more about you," he said.

"Lewis, you were searching for someone to make your fantasies come true, you were never interested in me. You were only interested in what I was doing to you and with you," she continued.

"I am not denying that I wasn't physically attracted to you," he said.

"Lewis I could have never been more than a sex partner to you, after I would have fulfilled all that you needed you would have started looking else where. What you did wasn't a mistake it's a character trait and it's just in you. You messed up when you screwed over a decent woman like Jasmine. You just completely disregarded your relationship and all that you two had invested in it," she said.

"So what does that say about you, it takes two to tango," he said.

"It says that I was horny and needed to be relieved and you came along. I got what I wanted and moved on. In other words you destroyed your relationship over something you would have never been able to keep," she said with a little laughter in her voice.

"You are a cold hearted bitch," he said.

"Well look at it this way at least your fantasies have come true, so ask yourself was it worth it? Was it worth losing the only woman who would probably have loved you with all she had and for what? For a fantasy that has ended, remember this Lewis just because it looks good doesn't mean that it's good for you. Take care I hope you find what you're looking for, before I let you go can you do me a favor?" she asked.

"Sure what's that," he said hoping that she would ask for one more night together.

"Please don't call me anymore I don't think my friend would appreciate that goodbye," she said.

"Friend?" he said aggressively.

"Hello, hello," he repeated until he heard a dial tone. Natalie had hung the phone up. As he sat there, staring at the telephone as if he couldn't believe what she did. He dialed her number again, this time the answering machine picked up.

"Natalie, I know you're there, pick up don't do this to me I need you right now," he slurred into the machine. Natalie had turned the volume down on the machine, knowing that he would call her back and besides his number was on the caller ID.

He sat there now, even more frustrated and lonely. He had no one to turn to his world had come crumbling down on him. Sitting there in his sorrow, he knew deep down inside, that she was right. He knew he had treated Jasmine wrong and was feeling all of her hurt and pain. He sat there and cried out, "What did I do, how could I have been so stupid?"

CHAPTER 11

Jasmine slept most of the evening away, unaware that it was late into the night. She put on her favorite song and lit her scented candles. She danced around the house; her thoughts were consumed with the possibility of seeing Anthony tomorrow. Time wasn't moving fast enough for her, she was looking forward to spending her evening at the massage parlor. Hoping that he would be there, since he was the one who sent her the gift certificate.

She visualized as much as she could about his features. She remembered that he was somewhere around six feet, muscular built with broad shoulders and his legs had a slight bow to them. She remembered that sight form the time he walked away from her on the beach. She was amazed at how his legs bowed that way. She was having thoughts, about the things she would love to do to him. Most importantly, where she would like those legs wrapped. She remembered the way he stared into her eyes, with his big brown eyes that always seemed to be glossy.

She fell onto the sofa, closed her eyes and remembered how he held her in his arms as they danced in the sand. How a stranger could come and sweep her away in one night, making her feel so secure. She smiled as she thought about the way she fit under his chest and nestled there, feeling his heart beating rapidly. Her hands began to slide over her stomach, the more she thought about that night the more she began to get aroused. Her back arched as she tried to so hard to fight the urge of getting her self worked up into a frenzy. Her heart began to pound and her eyes closed tighter as the fire began to burn inside. She felt the flames getting hotter and hotter with every thought of him. Amazed that Anthony had truly turned her world around with the mere thought of anticipation.

The telephone rung, unfazed by the rings Jasmine continued to stay in her zone. It's been a while since she had felt like this. "Hello! This is Anthony I was just calling to see," he said before Jasmine jumped up and grabbed the telephone. She tried not to sound as if she was just caught up in a moment of ecstasy.

"Hi stranger, how have you been? Thank you for the flowers and the card," she said.

"You're welcome I wanted to do something to let you know that I was thinking of you and how that night was so amazing. I have never met a woman with intelligence accompanied by beauty, sensuality and a passion for romance," he said in deep voice.

"Thank you," she said as a huge smile came over her face. "I have been wondering what happened to you," she asked.

I have been here and there trying to handle my business. I figured I would let our night marinate a little just to keep things in perspective," he said.

"I was just sitting here thinking about you, I'm glad to see that you're doing well," she said.

"Thoughts of you were always on my mind, every time I closed my eyes there you were as beautiful as ever," he said.

Hearing his voice was making Jasmine body tingle with excitement, as she felt the fire inside her begin to light back up. She made her way to her room and closed the door to eliminate as much light as she could. She was not going to let this moment pass by, the moment where she could let her inner passion run free. Anthony contin- ued talking, she responded with short an- swers as she got herself together for her moment. She began luring him into her trap, like lovers to stars.

"Anthony tell me how you felt about that night when we were on the beach," she asked.

"Jasmine I hear it in your voice," he said.

"Here what?" she said feeling embar- rassed.

"I hear the wanting of release in your voice, I can help you if you want I don't mind and please don't be ashamed of it," he said seductively.

"I feel so ashamed, how could you have known?" she asked.

"I just know…but that's not important, what's important is you right now and only you. So let me steer this ride and you just enjoy the trip, if that's okay with you?" he asked with a little laughter.

"Sure!" she said without hesitation.

"Close your eyes and listen to my voice pay attention to my instructions and I'll take you on an erotic journey, it doesn't work if you hold back. Will you let go and let me have control of your inner being for only a few minutes?" he asked.

"Yes!" she responded.

"I want you to picture yourself coming home from a hard day at work, I'll greet you at the door and signal for you, not to make a sound. I want you to just follow me, as I grab you by the hand and lead you to the bathroom. Awaiting you is a bubble bath filled with hot water to your liking. All the lights are off; the only source of light will be the flames from the scented candles burning. Now walk with me in your mind on this one, I want you to get up and go run some bath water," he said.

"Right now or are you just talking?" she asked.

"Yes right now you said you would allow me to take you on this journey and you said you would do as I asked, so I'm asking you to run the water," he said.

She agreed to go through with it, curious to see how it was going to turn out. She was ready to do what ever she needed to, to get the feeling that's inside her tamed.

"Okay the water is running, what's next?" she asked.

"Now get the candles and turn off the lights, get in the tub when it's finished running, no need to talk to me just listen and enjoy," he directed.

Jasmine's heart began to beat rapidly as thoughts of how he had complete dominance over her. No man had ever taken her mind beyond the point of losing control, but she had no complaints so far. She patiently awaited the next set of instructions and what he wanted her to do.

"Is the water ready?" he asked.

"Yes, it is," she responded.

"Okay, splash it around for me," he asked.

Jasmine took her hand and splashed the water around creating more bubbles. "Okay, now will you allow me to come over and complete the rest of this journey?" he asked.

Shocked by the question Jasmine got even more excited at the thought of seeing him, especially seeing him in the state of mind that she was. Jasmine was feeling vulnerable and would have been willing to do anything in the name of pleasure. Pausing for a moment, she agreed to let him come over. She gave him the directions and tried to pull out of him some information about his intent. Not giving any information or clues about his plan, he continued to give her instructions.

"I will need for you to either leave the door open or place the door keys somewhere I can get to them," he told her.

"Leave my keys out?" she responded sounding concerned.

"I would like to come in and not interrupt your bath and besides I am in control," he said with laughter.

"I will leave the key under the door mat, just make sure you leave it on the table before you leave," she responded.

"Sure no problem," he said. Confirming the directions, he hung up and she commenced to get in the tub and let her body marinate in the hot soothing water. She laid back allowing the bubbles to cover her completely. Closing her eyes, she drifted away on a memory bliss. Anthony finally arrived he entered the apartment, glanced around noticing that it was well decorated. He was impressed by her taste, but he wasn't expecting anything less. He prepared the other half of her fantasy evening, smiling because he knew that she had no clue of what was about to happen to her. He made his way down the hallway to the bathroom, assuming the closed door was the one he gently knocked on it.

"Jasmine it's me Anthony, may I enter?" he asked.

Lying there now feeling nervous, she hadn't seen or spoke to him in two weeks and here he was at her bathroom door. Her emotions were running wild and she couldn't believe that he was actually there. Well she figured that this is the moment of truth was he really going to take her on a erotic journey or was he going to be a built up hype that didn't pan out. There was only one way to find out and that was to continue what they started.

"Come in," she said.

Entering slowly allowing the candlelight to glisten off his sculpted body, he was wearing a pair of silk pants and slippers. As he made his way completely into the bathroom, his body consumed the entire surrounding. The only thing she could see was the shape of his body, she couldn't help but notice the way his stomach rippled and his chest protruded his body. She looked him up and down, noticing from the bulge in his pants; he wasn't wearing any underwear. She closed her eyes, trying so hard to keep her cool and not let him know how unraveled she was. He walked over and picked up the towel indicating that it was time to come to him. Nervous about getting out, this was the first time he had seen her naked.

"What if he doesn't like my body?" she asked herself.

Slowly rising out of the tub, she noticed how his eyes inspected her from head to toe. His eyes connected with hers, from the look in his eyes she knew he was pleased by what he saw. He gently turned her around so he could wrap her in the towel. She melted in his arms as they brushed seductively passed her. Ensuring that the towel was secured around her, he placed her hand in his and guided her to the living room. The atmosphere was like a scene out of a harlequin movie. Her eyes were drawn to the teacup candles that surrounded a velvet blanket sprinkled with rose pedals. To the side, there was a bottle of oil and something that resembled a handkerchief, not asking any questions she continued to follow him. He guided her over to the blanket and gently escorted her to the floor. Removing the towel from around her, he motioned her to lie on her stomach. He laid next to her, giving her some comfort; he noticed from the way she tightened her legs together she was very nervous.

"It's going to be okay Jasmine, I will be gentle and trust me things aren't always what they look like," he whispered in her ear.

"What you think is going to happen isn't but rest assure that your body will never be the same after tonight," he said as he kissed her on the ear.

He sat up and grabbed the bottle of scented oil, poured it in his hands first to warm it so she wasn't shocked by the touch. He placed his hands on her shoulders massaging them firm but gentle, he realized that her legs were no longer gripped together. He continued to introduce his fingers to all of her body parts, ensuring that every part got equal attention. The manipulation went on for about an hour finishing with her on her back, he reached down and grabbed the piece of cloth that laid there abandon serving no purpose, but now it will. Jasmine gasped at the thought of the cloths purpose, she was afraid of being blind folded.

"Anthony, please don't blind fold me, I'm claustrophobic," she pleaded.

"There are two combinations that are perfect together and that's fear and pleasure. I assure you that you will forget all about the blindfold, in a few minutes and allow the pleasure to take over," he said trying to reassure her.

"If I don't like it will you promise to stop?" she asked.

"I doubt that you would want me to stop, but if you do want me to I will," he responded with a smile on his face.

"Hold on Jasmine now your journey is about to begin," he said. He placed the cloth over her eyes as he guided her back down; he waved his hand over her face to ensure that she couldn't see. He turned the music up a little to enhance her fear. He lay next to her giving her some comfort, as he took his hand and began stroking her thighs. He blew in her ear sending a chill throughout her entire body, she knew from that moment on that she was going to be in for a long evening.

Jasmine was no longer in the mood to fight her feelings; she was at the point of no return. She now knew that he was doing a good job at steering this ride and she was going to enjoy being the passenger. He continued to do as he pleased to her. He kissed her on the ear and began to explore parts of her body that has been on vacation for a long time. He parted her legs receiving no resistance from her, he slid his hand as far up as he could meeting a point where his hand could go no further. With sensual strokes he found the password allowing his fingers to pass in, after entering he realized that he wasn't prepared for the moisture that followed. Aroused by the response of his entrance he began to simultaneously kiss her along the nape of her neck. The more his fingers introduced her to parts of her anatomy that she never knew existed; her voice seemed to come alive.

Just as he predicted she had completely forgotten about being blindfolded and was swept away in his world. Allowing her passion to be released a multitude of times, drained her to the point that she no longer had energy to move. She begged him to stop, unable to handle any more of his treatment. Jasmine realized that her body had been pushed to limits beyond her wildest imagination. Amazed that all this could take place without even having intercourse, afraid to even think where her mind and body would be if that was included.

He wrapped his arms around her allowing her to snuggle next to him. Looking over at him as he lay there with his eyes closed as if he had instantly dozed off. She couldn't help but wonder what would it be like to have him in her life permanently, or was he just someone there to bring her inner passions to life. Either way it went it didn't bother her. He was all hers for that moment. Enjoying the sight of him a little longer, she too drifted off into her dream world. They fell asleep in each other's arm without saying a word; the night ended.

CHAPTER 12

The light from the morning sun made its way through the cracks in the blinds, finding a home on her face. Jasmine rolled over trying to reset her body next to Anthony's, but she greeted by an empty space. She awoke in her bed, but remembered falling asleep on the living room floor.

"He was so sweet for carrying me to bed." She called out his name, "Anthony," hoping he had made his way to another part of the house, "Anthony," but there was no response. She got out of the bed; her body having a hang over from all the things he physically and emotionally put her through. Drinking a couple glasses of champagne didn't help either. She knew it was a well-deserved work out and couldn't wait to do her follow-up training. She made her way to the bathroom, looked in the mirror, smiling about last night's event. She realized that there was something different, her body felt lighter. Almost as if she had released a thousand pounds of pressure off her back. Jasmine stood in the mirror admiring her glow and her newfound energy. Nothing in the world could change the feeling. Making her way into the living room to reminisce about last night, she was not looking forward to cleaning up the mess they made. She remembered trying to escape the pleasure of his touch causing her to knock over one of the end tables. There was no way she was going to stop and clean anything up, she figured she would end up knocking it over again.

She entered the living room where she was greeted by an awkward sight; there was no mess. She walked around and noticed that everything was back in its original place. No sign that anything even took place no smell of intimacy, scented candles or him. The end table she remembered knocking over, was in its normal spot, even the pencil that was on it was back in its place. She walked over to the counter to see if her key was there and it was, but it was back on her key chain. She knew she wasn't dreaming it was real. She remembered running her hands across his face and touching every inch of his body. She went to the kitchen to see if the glasses they used for wine were in the sink. There were no sign of any glasses being used. She tried not to be wrapped up in it; she passed it off, as he cleaned up everything before he left. Anyway, today was the day that she receives her royal treatment at the Fantasy Massage Parlor. She looked at the clock to check the time. It was it was a little past noon and she had to get moving because time was flying by. The phone startled her, she ran over to it hoping to hear Anthony's voice.

"Hello," she said trying to sound sexy.

"Hello this is Marie from the Fantasy Massage Parlor is Ms Simmons in?" the operator responded.

"This is she," she said.

"I was calling to confirm your appointment for tonight, you are scheduled for the Ultimate Hawaiian Package, being picked up at 4:45pm this evening at 51 Sanders St is this correct?" she asked.

"Yes! That is correct," she responded.

"Are there any questions before I let you go?" she asked.

"No! None at this time," Jasmine said.

"Again we are looking forward to seeing you; you will enjoy every moment, see you soon goodbye," Marie said as she hung up.

She smiled as she walked off, like a little kid coming out of a candy store. She started to do her Saturday cleaning ritual, since the place was already clean, the only thing left for her to do was wash her clothes and straighten up her closet. She was so engulfed in her chores that she forgot about the time. She had to start getting dressed. The limousine will be there soon and she had no clue as to what she was going to wear. She pulled out something casually sexy, hopped in the shower and got dressed. Just as she finished her makeup, there was a knock at the door. She went and opened the door; there stood the driver a tall man dressed in a black and white tuxedo. It was hard to see his face; the way he wore his hat gave him that mystery appeal. She was going to be very suspicious today, wondering when or if Anthony was going to surprise her. Jasmine smiled from the excitement, she couldn't believe that the day had come and it was really happening.

"Please come in, I will be a few seconds I need to do some finishing touches to my hair and I will be ready," Jasmine asked.

"Thank you but if its okay ma'am, I will wait for you at the limousine," he responded.

"Sure! It will only take a second and I will be right out," she responded. Acknowledging her response he turned and walked off.

She finished her hair, gathered her things and headed out the door. She closed the door, the telephone rings. She stopped, looked at the door turned and kept going she was already running late. She closed the door and headed towards the limousine. Her answering machine picked up. "Hi! You've reached 555-2121 sorry I'm not in to take your call at this time so leave a message at the tone and I will get back to you," the machine said.

"Jasmine if you're there pick up this is Lewis, I need to talk to you. I know what you're doing tonight, I was hoping that you wouldn't go and maybe we could have dinner or something, you know maybe work us out?" he said. The message time elapsed and he was cut off, determined to win her over, he called back continuing to speak into the machine.

Jasmine was now on her way to the limousine. As she made her way to the car, the driver opened her door. A male dressed in nothing but a straw wrap, matching headpiece and sandals exited the limo. He stood approximately six feet two inches and his body was very muscular. She noticed the barbwire tattoos that circled his huge biceps. He walked up to her, held out his arms and escorted her to the car.

"Hello Ms. Simmons my name is Poi I will be your guide through your Hawaiian Fantasy, anything you need don't hesitate to ask," he said.

Unable to speak she nodded her head and continued to marvel at the sight of this male specimen in front of her. They both entered the car, the driver closed the door behind them, and they drove off. She sat there and looked around the limo, besides Poi, her ears were attracted to the Hawaiian music being played and the sound of a blender going off.

"Pina Colada or strawberry dacari non alcoholic of course?" he asked.

"Pina Colada thanks," she said.
He poured the drink into a coconut turned glass, with an umbrella straw.

"Here you go Ms. Simmons I hope you enjoy it," he said.

She sipped it and returned her approval with a smile; she sat back in the seat enjoying the drink and music. Minutes passed by and the arrival to the parlor was nearing, she could feel the excitement in her bones.

"We're almost there, if you're finished with the drink I will take it for you. You'll get the glass back at the end of your get-away as a souvenir," he said.

The limousine pulled in front of the parlor. From the outside it gave a mysterious appearance with the smoked windows. Her heart raced, she was anxious to get inside, to see why there was so much hype. The driver opened the door, Poi and Jasmine exit the car and entered the building.

"Follow me," Poi said.

They walked into the building; he motioned her to have a seat, and then disappeared behind a door. She sat in a plain room no paintings, no decorations, just six chairs and the door her escort used to leave the room. She was feeling strange. There was no music, she figured there would at a minimum be a receptionist. Minutes passed then the door opened and a lady came out.

"Welcome to The Fantasy Massage Parlor, the ultimate getaway, follow me please," she said in an angelic voice. "Ms. Simmons this is your private dressing room, inside you'll find a pair of slippers, a robe and a lock-box for your personal goods. When you have undressed and placed on the robe, come out the door we entered and I will be waiting for you," she said.

"I'll only be a few minutes," Jasmine responded.

Jasmine watched her as she walked in a direct manner out the door. She looked around her room, finding a plush white robe folded on a chair. She picked it up held it next to her body; it went from her neck to her ankles. It had the initials FM in black letters on the left breast pocket. She sat down on the beautiful white wicker chair with overstuffed cushions and cuddled her robe. She had never felt anything so soft. She reached down and picked up the matching slippers. She took her shoes off and slid her feet in them. They were equally as soft as the robe.

"I sure hope these come with the souvenir glass," she said jokingly.

She finished getting undressed and put on the robe and the slippers. She smiled at the feeling of the material on her skin. She pulled her curtain shut and made her way out the door and back to the lobby. Her escort was there waiting to take her to the next phase.

"How is everything so far?" the escort asked.

"Everything is fine," Jasmine responded.

"Through these doors your fantasy will begin..are you ready?" she asked.

"Yes I am," Jasmine said anxiously.

The escort opened the door and motioned her to enter. Jasmine noticed that the whole room was white, the carpet, walls employee uniforms and the equipment.

"Well Ms. Simmons this is as far as I go, enjoy. Amber will take over from here," she said as she closed the door behind her. Jasmine turned back around to marvel at the room she was in, when a lady dressed in white walked up to her.

"Hello Ms. Simmons please follow me to the nail technician where you will be given a manicure and a pedicure," she said as she turned and walked away. Jasmine followed her over to a section of the room designated for doing nails.

"Please have a seat, Raymond will be right with you," she asked.

"Raymond?" she responded shockingly.

"Yes we have found that most women prefer to be pampered by a man and he is one of the best, trust me you will enjoy it," she said as she walked off.

A tall slim almost malnutritioned gentleman turned the corner; he walked with style and sophistication. His hair was pulled back in a ponytail and his white outfit was freshly pressed, with matching white leather square-toed shoes.

"Hello Ms. Simmons, my name is Raymond and I will be giving you your manicure and pedicure this evening. If you will, have a seat right here. I would normally turn on the chair's vibration system, since you're scheduled for a massage is it alright if I leave it off?" he asked.

"Sure that's fine."

"French manicure for both hands and feet?" he asked.

"You read my mind," she said. Jasmine sat back in the leather chair and allowed him to work his magic. He was so good at what he did, that when he started the pedicure, she dozed off. Time passed...when she awoke her hands and feet were finished.

"I feel better already, if this is all the treatment I get today I would be satisfied," she said.

"I'm glad you enjoyed it, it was nice meeting you," he said as he turned and walked off without saying another word.
Amber walked up with a big smile on her face, "How was everything, was he great or what?"

"Yes, he was very good," Jasmine responded.

"Okay Ms. Simmons it's time for your facial if you would, follow me please," she asked.

"There's more?" Jasmine asked.

"I was directed to not give you any clues as to what is going to happen. Well here's your next stop, Keith will take care of you from here, enjoy," she said as she again turned and walked off.

"Hello! Ms. Simmons welcome I will be giving you your facial this evening," he said.

She was caught off guard by Keith's physique; he looked nothing like a facial technician. He was built like a linebacker for a NFL team.

"I'm sorry for staring at you, but you just don't look like you do facials," she said.

"I get that all the time, it doesn't bother me. A friend of mine got me into this some years ago, after I hurt my knee-playing ball. I know it's a drastic career change, but the money is good," he said laughing at his comment. "Well Ms. Simmons it's time to get started, lay back here and I will take good care of you."

Jasmine followed his commands. Just as she did when her pedicure began, she dozed off. Time passed, and again she was awakened out of her nap.

"You're finished," he said as he handed her a mirror.

"Wow! My skin looks and feels so different," she remarked as she admired her face.

"Enjoy the remainder of your getaway the best is yet to come," he said.

"I will, thank you," she said.
He turned and walked away and Amber returns admiring her facial.

"You are glowing Ms. Simmons, how was your facial?" she asked.

"I love it he was very good. I feel like a new person," Jasmine remarked.

"Well, it's now time for your ultimate pampering, follow me please," she said as she turned and walked down a white hallway. They stopped in front of a white door, with the words Hawaii written on it.

"Behind this door is your fantasy, enter when you're ready," she said as she turned and again walked away.

Jasmine stood there with a little nervousness, hoping to find Anthony on the other side. She figured he would show up eventually, since she hadn't seen him all afternoon. She took a deep breath and exhaled slowly trying to relax her racing heart. She turned the doorknob and entered the room. Gasping at the sight, the room was beautiful, it had all the features of Hawaii minus the sand. The walls were all painted like a tropical view there was a huge aquarium in the wall with colorful tropical fish, the ceiling was painted like the sunset, and it was a beautiful room. The music was so soothing; it was a mellow Hawaiian tune coming from the ceiling. Entering this room after being in all that white made her feel like she walked into a dream. The door opened and her masseuse entered.

"Hello Ms. Simmons I will be your masseuse for the next hour. If you would please slip on this towel and lay on the table and your massage will begin shortly," he said.

"How do you want me to lay on the table, on my back or my stomach?" she asked.

"On your stomach please, I will be back momentarily," he said.

She placed the towel over her and lay down on the table. The door opened and entered Anthony. He dimmed the lights, turned the music up and the massage was now about to begin. He took the oil and began to rub his hands together he observed his starting point and placed his hands there. He began stroking her skin with great precision, like a painter to his picture. Jasmine noticed her body's reaction to his strokes. Her fire was beginning to ignite. Her heart is pounding, she realized that there was something different about this masseuse. The more he manipulated her muscles the more her loins reacted. She tried not to give in to the feelings.

She closed her eyes trying to block out the sensations. She had a feeling it was Anthony, but she knew if she turned over and it wasn't him, how embarrassing that would be. She was fighting the urge with everything she had to not turn around and look. With every unique stroke came a different level of goose bumps. She could feel the juices overflow its cup and she knew that she would explode at any moment. Time was passing by and she was mentally drained from the touches of this stranger, but somehow the touches didn't seem strange. There was a pause, the strokes had stopped and then they started back up. Her body went into shock, the hands were different and the strokes were less sensual. She had a feeling there was a change in masseuse.

"Your hour is up now Ms. Simmons," he said. Jasmine turned and to her surprise, she found her original masseuse standing over her.

"Is everything okay?" he asked.

"Yes everything is fine, the massage was great an experience that I will never forget," she responded.

"I'm glad you enjoyed it, I will see you later," he said as he walked out the room.

Amber entered with a cheerful smile, noticing the puzzled look on Jasmine's face.

"You look disturbed Ms. Simmons, is everything okay?" she asked.

"Yes I am just amazed at the massage it was overwhelming, I have never felt like that before. Well maybe once, it was almost like déjà vu," Jasmine said.

"I take it that's a good thing?" Amber asked.

"Yes it is," Jasmine returned with a smile. They continued to laugh about it, as Amber escorted her to the dressing room. Jasmine changed into her clothes and returned to the lobby. She was greeted by the staff. They hugged her and thanked her for coming. She left the building. The limousine was parked out front waiting for her departure. On the ride home she sat back in the seat, mesmerized at the whole evening. The ride home was a bit quieter than the ride to the parlor. She figured it was designed to keep you in that relaxed mode. They finally arrived back at her place. She exited the vehicle and was given a package and a lei was placed around her neck. The driver watched her as she entered her apartment, then drove off into the night.

Jasmine sat on her sofa, opened her package and smiled at the contents. There was the robe, the slippers, and coconut glass. A piece of cloth in a plastic bag with the words "smell me on it." She opened the bag and it was Anthony's cologne, the same scent he left on the paper when they first met. She knew deep down inside that Anthony had given her that massage. She got undressed and prepared for bed; she was well relaxed from her evening and knew she was finally going to have a good night's rest. She wrapped herself in the robe, crawled into bed and dosed off into a deep sleep.

CHAPTER 13

The weekend went by just as fast as it came and getting up for work seemed harder than normal. She lay in the bed for a moment staring at the ceiling, thinking about her weekend and the relaxation she had. She couldn't believe how much of her fantasy had come true since meeting Anthony. He was everything she wanted in a man. He was attractive, intriguing, a good conversationalist and extremely romantic. Their meeting, the beach, the surprise at work and the massage parlor, no one had ever treated her the way he had. She was having fun, but something was beginning to bother her.

"Why all the mystery? This entire secret stuff. What is he hiding?" she questioned herself. She was enjoying everything, but things weren't adding up.

Her body and mind was in another time zone and she was trying desperately to get distracted by those thoughts. Her alarm clock buzzed, quickly returning her to reality and that was getting ready for work. She turned the radio on to her favorite morning talk show, on WTFM FM 90.1.

"Today we have Dr. Baxter with us to talk about her new book, Relationships. Welcome," Tom the radio personality said.

"Thank you, I'm glad to be on your show this morning," she said.

"So tell us a little about this book," Tom asked.

"The book basically talks about some situations relationships go through, when they go from intimacy to friendship, instead of friendship to intimacy. It deals with the process of how they come together and how they end, if not done in the correct order. It also touches on the involvement of friends and family, and how they affect a relationship," she said.

Jasmine stopped and focused on the radio conversation; she thought how ironic the topic was. Her thoughts were quickly turned to Renee and the talk she needed to have with her. She turned off the radio, she knew it was distracting her and she didn't want to be late for work. She finished getting dressed and rushed out to her car hoping to catch the tail end of the show. By the time she got situated in the car, the doctor was off the air. It wasn't a loss; it helped her remember the talk she needed to have with Renee. Today was the day she was going to confront her about her actions and how she was feeling betrayed. It wasn't about seeing her and Lewis together, but the fact she allowed their personal conversations to be shared with him.

Renee was her best friend and it hurt her to have to be going through this. She knew that Renee and Lewis were friends. She was the one that introduced them. She figured the hugging, she saw them doing could have been her consoling him. The thing that puzzled her the most, was the fact she was giving him all this information about her personal life. If she was seeing him, she was in violation of the best friend law. That is you never mess with someone your friend was with or had interest in. The thought of Lewis being with someone else wasn't the case, but being with Renee was and to lose her friend over a man would devastate her. Especially, if it was for her ex-boyfriend. Therefore, she knew that the day wouldn't end until she spoke with her face to face. She was going to try to be positive about the whole thing or she could be blowing the situation out of proportion.

There was something deep down inside her that made her think differently though.

Renee sat at her desk wondering how Jasmine's weekend went. She knew she was going to the massage parlor for her getaway package. She was feeling a little jealous about the treatment Jasmine was receiving. Why was it that she got all the fun, she herself had suffered some bad relationships, but she never ended up with a guy like Anthony? The more she sat there and thought about it, the more anger grew. Since Jasmine didn't call her this weekend to tell her about the event, she figured that their friendship was at it's end and that she had a new friend in Anthony. Well she wasn't going to just let her drop her so easily; she had something in mind to make her perfect world crumble. She picked up the phone and called Lewis, hoping he was still at home since it was his day off.

"Hello," he said.

"Hello it's me, what are you doing?" she asked.

"Nothing much just sitting here waiting for my clothes to dry, what's on your mind?" he asked.

"I want to see you tonight at my place around nine o'clock ok?" she asked.

"I can't do it I have to work tonight," he said.

"I really need to see you tonight we have to talk," she said with desperation in her voice.

"What's going on Renee?", he asked with a concerned voice.

"I need to see you I want to do something tonight," she said.

"Do what?" he said.

"You know what I want and I want it tonight," she demanded.

"I can't. I am trying to win Jasmine back, I thought you were helping me do that?" he asked.

"Lets get one thing straight when I introduced you two, you and I were doing our own thing and we agreed that as long as I wanted some you would give it to me. You know mister have your cake and eat it too, so what's with the technicalities now?" she asked.

"I have really begun to fall in love with her, that's the technicality," he responded.

"Were you in love with her last week when we were sweating up your sheets, when you were laying on your floor looking and sounding pathetic?" she asked.

"Yes! I was, I was just confused and needed a friend and you were there for me," he responded.

"Were you in love when you asked me to hook you up with my girl?" she asked.

"Were you in love when you participated in that threesome, by the way I have it on video or did you forget that part too? Remember when you came to me complaining that Jasmine wouldn't make any of your fantasies come true and I told you I would and I did? Well now it's your turn to be there for me," she continued.

"What if I don't do this?" he asked.

"I'm sure you know the outcome, this tape will end up in her mailbox and any chance you may have had will be gone," she said.

"Well Lewis, it's your choice I don't have all day, you think about it and let me know and, oh yeah, I will leave you with this thought. There are some fantasies that are best left in your mind, not all are good for you," she said with a slick laughter.

"I will be there but this will be it, no more after this okay?" he asked.

"This will be it, I promise," she responded.

"Before we hang up I have a question to ask you," he responded.

"Yes what is it?" she said.

"It's obvious that Jasmine and I are through, but what about your friendship, she is your best friend does that mean anything to you?" he asked.

"In her eyes I was her best friend, she was never my best friend, I did use her as I used you to fulfill my fantasies and now I have accomplished them. Tonight will be the end of my fantasy and I will no longer need you or her, but don't think about not showing up remember I still have the video," she said.

"Like I said I will be there and I want the tape and that's that. After tonight I don't ever want to see you again," he said.

"Don't worry you won't," she responded.

"Nine o'clock just be there ready to perform for me, one last time," she said as she hung up the phone.

He knew he could never tell Jasmine about this or his chance at ever winning her back would be over. The only thing he could do was show up and handle his business. Then leave and never look back. Besides he had nothing to lose, he would be damned if he did and damned if he didn't. The only choice he had was to go and ensure that she was thoroughly satisfied and get a hold of that tape.

If he can get the tape back he could again focus on getting Jasmine back, without the threat of his past haunting him. He finally got up out of the chair and continued getting himself together. Since there was a change in his plans, he now had to alter his schedule and call in using one of his sick days. Hoping that this night would end it all and he could finally move on with his life.

CHAPTER 14

Jasmine's day had finally ended and Renee hadn't called her all day. No matter what was going on in their lives whether good or bad, she always called. The situation was more serious than she expected; whatever it was she hoped they would work through it. Jasmine made it home, changed clothes and cooked a light dinner. She finished the remainder of her paper work she had to bring home from the office. She glanced up at the time and realized it was now 8:30 p.m. and she really wanted to talk to Renee tonight. She tried calling her, but there was no answer. Maybe she was screening her calls and didn't want to talk to her, she thought to herself. It really didn't matter because this conversation was going to take place one way or another.

She got herself together, snatched her purse off the counter and headed out the front door. She arrived at the entrance to

Renee's complex and pulled over to get her thoughts together. She didn't want to go in there making claims that may not be true. This was her best friend she was talking about, someone whom she would trust with her life. If she went in there making accusations it could mean the end of their friendship and she didn't want that to happen. She reminisced about the times when they would sit on a hill as kids, overlooking the highway.

Looking at the cars as they drove pass, claiming the one they wanted to buy. They talked about their future-plans, when they graduate from high school. They were planning to move away from the small town in Alabama and go to a college in a big city. That all changed when Renee's father had to transfer to California, because of a promotion. She hadn't seen Renee in years, until recently reuniting with her a year ago at a street festival in the heart of the city. She knew that time brings about a change in people, but she didn't want to believe that Renee changed. Jasmine wanted her old friend from back home, to still be that same person. To her Renee was always her best friend. She sat in her car for a few minutes, getting her questions together. Jasmine's main concern was, why the sudden distance and coldness she had placed between them. What did she do or wasn't doing to cause this to be happening? Either way it went it was time to go through with it, if she was at home.

She turned the corner and there her car was. She figured she was either out with someone else or just not answering her phone. She pulled in to park when she noticed another familiar car in one of the parking spaces. The tags were a dead give-away LEWIS1, her heart began to pound and her blood began to boil.

"What in the world is he doing here? Well this would work out perfectly, I can kill two birds with one stone," she said to herself.

She turned towards the apartment and begun to walk up to the door, when she realized that there were no lights on. She knocked on the door, but there was no answer or any sound of life. She attempted to call her from her cell phone and again no answer just the machine. Something inside her was telling Jasmine that her worst fears were about to come true. She tried the door handle to see if it was unlocked, it was. How careless could she be leaving her door unlocked?

Jasmine entered the apartment finding clothes in the doorway; there was a combination of male and female clothing covering the entranceway. Jasmine's eyes began to fill as she realized the reality of her findings. Her heart couldn't take another let down. She walked down the hallway, following the sounds of his and her voices, with passion as the back-up singer. The aroma of sex filled the air and the continuous sound of skin colliding into each other made her nauseous. She was afraid to enter the room to find them together, but the fact was, they were.

She opened the door and there they were tangled in each other's arms like a woven blanket. She turned on the lights and stood there watching them scurry apart. She looked at Renee with a blank expression on her face, standing there motionless. She was unable to say anything. If looks could kill she would be facing a double murder charge. Jasmine looked over at Lewis and gave him a halfway smile of disgust.

To make matters worst, the bathroom door opened and out walked Natalie wrapped in a sleazy outfit resembling something of a hooker.

"Don't finish without me," she said as she walked out not noticing Jasmine in the doorway.

Renee motioned towards the door, telling Natalie to look in that direction.

"Oh! Are you here to participate?" Natalie asked as she climbed in the bed.

"How could you do this to me you're my best friend, I trusted you with everything I had. I loved you like you were my sister and I would have done anything for you. I was always there for you when you needed someone to laugh with, talk with and cry with," she said to Renee.

"Jasmine so much about me had changed when I left Alabama. I left so much of that life behind me. You saw me as the old Renee. I thought it was cool seeing you again, but that's not me anymore. You know Jasmine you never once asked me, what has been going on in my life since I left. You were only concerned with talking about back home and our childhood. Had you asked, you probably wouldn't be standing there looking stupid," she said with a criminal smile.

Jasmine stood there speechless wanting so much to jump in the bed and just beat her until she couldn't beat her no longer. She kept her composure, looked over at

Lewis and said, "I would have forgiven you in time Lewis. You just wouldn't give me time to deal with anything. I could be childish and call you all kinds of things, but it won't change anything. What goes around comes back around and you'll have it coming, one way or another," she said calmly as she turned and ran out the apartment.

"Jasmine! Jasmine wait," he yelled as he gathered his clothes to run after her. It was to late she had made it to her car and was pulling off by the time he made it to the parking lot. He turned to go back to the bedroom to confront Renee.

"Are you happy now? Look at what you did," he said.

"What I did? It was your fantasy Lewis this is what you asked for wasn't it?" she asked.

"It wasn't suppose to be like this, she wasn't suppose to know," he said.

"Well just think your fantasies have been fulfilled and at what cost were you willing to pay for it?" she asked.

"Was it worth losing everything for a piece of ass Lewis? Now you're no longer welcomed in this bed. I'm sure you're not welcomed in her bed either," she said with laughter as she turned and kissed Natalie.

"You set me up? You caused me to be caught by Jasmine at work with Natalie, didn't you?" he questioned.

Renee just looked and smiled at him. "Hold your finger up Natalie, you see that tattoo on her finger…that means she is mine and you see the tattoo on my finger that means that I am hers. You see Lewis, you too played a part in our fantasy. Now that it's all in the open, there's no use for you anymore. Unless you plan to watch, I would suggest that you leave before I call the cops. Close the front door for me on your way out please," she asked as she turned and continued tending to Natalie.

He stood there in the door with rage building up, but he knew it wouldn't be worth it to do anything to them. He turned and walked out of the apartment, leaving the door wide open. He hopped into his car and tried contacting Jasmine but there was no answer at her place. He knew that somehow he had to get a hold of her, knowing that she was in so much pain. He had to get to her and try to explain it all and apologize. He drove past her place but her car wasn't there and the lights were off, there was no sign of her. He drove home and tried to contact her again, just like his last attempts he got the answering machine.

"Jazzy I know you're there pick up please I need to explain this to you at least hear me out and I will never call you again," he begged into the machine.

He was right about one thing she was at home, laying on her bed crying uncontrollably, making herself sick. There was nothing he could have said to her, to ease her pain. He continued to talk until the machine cut him off. Jasmine needed someone to talk to, but she had no one. Her best friend had just betrayed her, the pain was unbearable and it hurt twice as much, as it did when she caught him with Natalie. She turned to pick up the phone to call Anthony, so he could help ease her pain and give her some comforting words. She waited for him to pick up, but there was a recording from the Phone Company.

"Sorry, you have reached a number that has been disconnected or is no longer in service."

Jasmine couldn't believe what she was hearing. Maybe she had dialed the wrong number. She dialed it again and again she received the same message. She hung the phone up and realized that she was truly alone. Unable to stay in the house she decided to go for a ride, to clear her mind. She walked down her hallway and glanced at the picture of her and Renee in their happier moments. She took the picture off the wall, frame and all and tossed it in the trash. She got into her car and drove around town. She drove to the café where she met Anthony, hoping that maybe she could experience deja-vu. Sitting there for a few minutes, she realized that he wasn't going to show up, so she drove off. She drove to the Fantasy Massage Parlor and to her surprise, the building was empty. There was a For Sale sign in the window, she got out the car to look in the building. The building was completely vacant; there was no indication that any such business existed. She got back into her car, sitting there in complete amazement.

This night couldn't be happening to her. She wondered what could she have possibly had done to deserve this treatment. Jasmine headed back home when her thoughts begin to reflect back over the night's events. Her eyes again began to fill with the all so familiar visit of tears. She just wanted to make it home, so she could climb into bed. At least try to get some sleep and deal with it in the morning. She arrived home checked her machine, which was filled with messages from Lewis. Not listening to any of them, she deleted them all. She attempted to contact Anthony one more time and again the same response from the phone company. She lay down on the bed and tried so hard to think about other things, but she couldn't shake the pain and continued to cry until she cried herself to sleep.

CHAPTER 15

Lewis sat on his floor with a bottle of cognac drinking it straight from the bottle, trying so desperately to deal with his emotions. Jasmine wasn't answering her phone, and he had no one to turn to. His relationship with Renee and Natalie was over and he had no other friends in the area. He paced the living room, with his hands interlocked behind his neck. The hurt in his heart was getting the best of him. Sweat rolled off his forehead onto his face, joining the tears that continued to stream down his cheeks. He sat on the carpet and picked up the photo album from the end table. He stared at the pictures, of the life he once shared with Jasmine.

They enjoyed so many good times together. His attention was drawn to a picture they took in Vegas. It was taken at a mock chapel, where they had pretended to be married. He remembered asking Jasmine if he'd proposed for real, would she have said yes. He recalled her grabbing his hands, looking him in his eyes and responding with, "Yes, I would Lewis."

He wanted so much for things to be the way they used to be, but he knew that they would never be able to be that way again. His mind started playing tricks on him; he began to believe he had no reason to live. He rubbed his hand over his heart, trying to calm the beating that raged in his chest. He attempted to pull himself off the floor but struggled, the alcohol was getting the best of him. He made his way to the kitchen table, gathered his thoughts the best he could. He turned on the radio, but there was nothing but slow songs playing; how fitting for this moment he thought. He sat there and continued to drink, listening to a song a man was singing, for his woman to come back home.

He could visualize Jasmine being with that Anthony guy tonight, wrapped tightly in his arms. That's probably why she wasn't answering her telephone. The more he thought about it, the more his heart began to cry out for her. He knew that if she was with him, he was the cause of it and could blame no one but himself. He knew he had to tell her everything or the truth would tear away at him. He pulled out his note pad and began to write her a letter. He was going to explain the whole story. He sat there for about an hour pouring out his heart, not holding anything back. At this point, he realized that he had nothing to lose. He wanted to take it to her personally, but he knew she wasn't up to seeing him and besides she may have company. Seeing her with another man would drive him insane, although he was caught with her best friend. That didn't matter to him, he figured men were allowed to do those things and should be forgiven. His father did it and he was forgiven, his mom didn't leave him. However, if a woman did it, she should have the scarlet letter placed on her back and paraded around town. He knew he was wrong for thinking that, but he was raised that way. Besides, it was a good excuse for him to justify her taking him back.

He played it safe and decided to go to the post office instead. He finished the letter, gathered his keys and headed out the door. He arrived at the post office, dropped the letter in the box and drove off. He went to a park where he and Jasmine used to take midnight walks and have picnics under the stars. The more he thought about it the more miserable he became, causing him to drink even more than before. The pain was getting the best of him; he couldn't believe how he had been treating Jasmine. The betrayal, the lies and the unfaithfulness, that was too much for one person to handle. His tears started falling with no sign of letting up. He backed up and then drove away. The more he thought about it, the more he consumed alcohol. He headed home with his thoughts still on Jasmine. His eyes were blurry and the only guides he had, were the warning bumps in the middle of the road. He placed the bottle on the seat, so he could reach for some tissue in the glove compartment. When he looked up, he was riding on the opposite side of the road. He could feel the ridges of the warning tracks against his tires.

His blurred eyes were greeted with bright flashing lights and the horn of the approaching vehicle rang in his ear. Trying to gain control of his car, he went off the road. He was going too fast to veer back onto the highway. The drinking impaired his ability to react. As his car headed towards the tree, his life flashed before him. He got the words, "Father God help me," out his mouth before his car made contact with a tree.

His car wrapped around the tree, as if it was hugging a long lost loved one. The sound of the crash echoed in the air, sending a sound of help to the heavens. His mangled car sat there, as cars passed by on the far side of the highway, unaware of his accident. His head rested on the top of the dashboard, after connecting with the windshield. His limp body laid dormant on the steering wheel. It was amazing that the impact didn't kill him instantly. Time passed by slowly as he lay there semi conscious, awaiting help.

Finally, off in the distance he vaguely heard a familiar sound, the sounds of emergency vehicles. Someone must have called the accident in. Barely able to see; unable to move, he couldn't tell if anyone was near him. The vehicles arrived and the sounds of urgency were all around. The opening from the shattered windshield, was all the officer needed so he could speak to Lewis.

"Hello, can you hear me?" he asked.

"Jas-mine?" he responded as blood rolled of his lips.

"It's going to be okay sir, we're going to get you out. Hang on you'll be out in a second," he said trying to comfort him.

"Tell her I'm sorry," he responded in a faint voice.

"Don't talk like that! Everything is going to be okay and you'll be able to tell her yourself," he said.

The officer stepped away from the car, allowing the Jaws of Life to do its job. They removed him from the damaged car, onto a stretcher. They began their emergency procedures, but they were racing against time. They could only administer first aide; his only chance for survival was getting him on the helicopter. The air medical transportation was nearing. The closer it approached the fainter his heartbeat got.

"You're going to be okay, hold on," the officer said as he watched him cough up more blood.

Lewis looked into his eyes, the best he could and said, "Re-mem-ber s-o-r-r-y," inhaling for the last time.

Jasmine was awakened by the sound of the telephone, she rolled over hoping to hear Anthony's voice on the other end, and it wasn't.

"Hello, is this Jasmine Simmons?" the officer asked.

"This is she may I help you," she responded in a sluggish voice.

"Yes, this is Sgt. Brown from the highway patrol, we need you to come down to the county hospital to identify a body," he stated.

"A body?" she asked as she sat up in her bed, wiping the sleep from her eyes.

"Your name was found on a card in this person's possession," he replied.

"Can you at least tell me whether this person is a man or women?" she asked.

"It was a male ma'am," he responded.

"What was the cause of death?" she asked

"A car accident ma'am, I will answer all your questions when you get here," he responded.

"I'll be right there," she said and hung up. She hopped out of bed and got dressed as fast as she could, throwing on the first things she could find. She headed towards the hospital and the only person on her mind was Anthony. She remembered giving him a business card when they first met, that's how he was able to send her the flowers. If it were Anthony, she was going to lose her mind. Losing everything in one night would be too much for her to handle. She didn't think she would be able to bear seeing him like that. She remembered the last time she saw him; they were enjoying each other's erotic ore. She was now faced with the possibility of viewing his body in a capacity that she never would have imagined. She picked up her cell phone to call Renee out of habit. She immediately closed the phone, realizing that they were no longer friends. Quickly putting the thoughts of Renee out of her mind, she redirected her thoughts back to the hospital and the vision that awaited her. Arriving at her destination, she pulled in the emergency room parking lot, trying to encourage herself.

"Okay Jasmine, you can do this, just get out and start walking," she said to herself.

She opened the door and climbed out, then she turned and climbed back in. She didn't have the strength to do it; she placed her head on the steering wheel and began to pray.

"Heavenly father, I come to you now in my darkest moment, I pray that the path you have placed before me is designed for you to get the glory. You said that you would place no more on me than I can bear, I stand firm on your word. Right now, I feel like David and a giant is awaiting me. I ask that you give me the spirit of David right now, give me the

courage to face this giant. I don't know how I'm going to make it through this without you. I ask that you touch me letting me know that you're here by my side. I need an emergency visit from you; I need you right now. You said that when two or three gather in your name, that you would be there. Right now, it's just you and I. I'm asking that you show up just for me."

Jasmine's face began to take form of a river; she was giving her all in this prayer. She was praying for more than what she was about to encounter at the hospital. Praying for her piece of mind and the strength needed to deal with the after affects of today. People walked by noticing the cries coming from her car, but continued to walk on. Jasmine tried to form words for her prayer, but they weren't coming out. She wasn't finished trying to reach God. She wanted to know that he was there with her and she wasn't going to stop until he showed up. She sat back in her seat and yelled at the top of her lungs, "Father God please help me!"

There was a tap on her window; Jasmine turned to find a woman standing about 5'6", full figured body frame. She was dressed very casual and had an odd look on her face. Jasmine rolled her window down to hear what she had to say.

"Yes! May I help you," she said as she tried wiping the tears from her eyes.

"I was walking by and I heard your cry. My name is Evangelist Harris," she said as she extended her hand out to her.

"My name is Jasmine," she answered as she accepted her greeting.

The evangelist held on to her hand longer than normal. Jasmine looked up at her, watching her close her eyes and began to take deep breaths. She turned to Jasmine and asked, "May I pray for you child?"

"Sure! Where do you want to do this at?" Jasmine asked.

"Right here, right now," the Evangelist said. She reached into her bag and pulled out a bottle of oil, she poured a little in her hand then placed the bottle back in the bag. Then she reached up rubbed a little on Jasmine's forehead. She grabbed both of Jasmine's hands and began her prayer ritual, she again started taking the deep inhales and slow exhales. She opened her eyes and looked into Jasmine's and the words that followed broke something in her.

"You're asking God for an emotional healing. You're facing a great task and you want to feel his presence. He had never left you. This is your time to seek him, call on him and believe. You are feeling like you have no one, oh she of little faith have you forgotten that he has the power to heal any pain or sickness. Oh she of little faith have you forgotten that he is the Alpha and the Omega the beginning and the end.

Joshua 1:9 says: Have I not commanded you? Be strong and of good courage; do not be afraid, nor be dismayed for the Lord your God is with you wherever you go. Stand up and walk with the strength he has embedded in you. You're seeking the spirit of David but God says that you have the spirit of Ruth in you. He said that when all things seems impossible he'll make it possible."

She placed Jasmine's head in her bosom and wrapped her arms around her, as if she was a long lost child making her way back home, into her mother's waiting arms. Jasmine felt her body getting weak and a feeling came over her that she had not felt in along time. The last time she had this feeling it was last year when she went to church and gave her life to God. She felt his presence; she felt his spirit in her bones. Tears flowed down her cheeks in an un-stoppable flow. They flowed so that they began to soak the Evangelist's blouse. Her body began to shake and the more she tried to stop crying she couldn't.

"It's okay let it all out he's here right now, welcome his presence, he knows that you love him," she said trying to comfort Jasmine.

Jasmine cried for a few more minutes, not caring about the people walking by staring at the two of them. She knew that God was there and didn't want to miss his visit. She wiped her tears and straightened up her face.

"Now go my child and leave all your burdens right here and don't pick them back up. God loves you; he will never leave you nor forsake you. Remember that no weapon formed against you shall prosper. As she embraced her, she whispered in her ear, "You're loved take care and stay encouraged."

She turned and without saying another word walked off into the parking lot. Jasmine wanted to see what she was driving, but she was lost in the sea of cars and was gone just as fast as she came. Her attention was turned back to the hospital by the sounds of an emergency vehicle pulling up to the building. She looked up to the night sky and gave thanks to the heavens, closed her car door and walked towards the entranceway. She walked up to the counter and talked to the nurse at the desk. She asked for directions to the officer that called her.

"Hi! I'm looking for Officer Brown," Jasmine inquired.

"Yes! Do you see that officer over by the book stand?" she asked.

"Yes! I do, thank you," Jasmine responded.

Jasmine walked toward him, he turned and instantly knew that she was the woman coming to identify the body.

"Ms. Simmons?" he asked.

"Yes!" she responded.

"I want you to know that what you're about to see is very graphic, I just need you to look at the body the best you can. The accident was very bad and the impact caused his body to get mangled in the car," he continued.

"We need you to ID this person, so we can put a closure to the case and notify his loved ones," he said with a sentimental tone.

"I don't know if I can do this," Jasmine responded.

"I know it is difficult, I will be right there by your side," he said trying to give her some reassurance that she wouldn't be alone.

"Take a few deep breaths," he asked.
Jasmine followed his instructions; at this point, she knew there was no turning back.

"Are you okay now, it's time to go in?" he said. They walked through the double doors, to a set of silver elevators. As they entered the elevators, Jasmine noticed the officer pressing the button with the word morgue next to it.

Instantly she started feeling nauseous from the fact that she had never seen a dead body before, let alone someone she may know. Even more so, someone that she may have been falling in love with. The elevator doors opened, the sight of this area was very gloom. You could tell by the atmosphere, that it was a place designed to accompany death. They turned left off the elevators and walked to the end of the hallway, where they stood at the entrance to a pair of swinging doors. The officer looked at Jasmine and noticed that she was already looking sick, but he had to get it over with. He knew how much pain she was in; he had seen it plenty of times. He knew there was nothing he could do for her. He opened the door, greeted the coroner and explained to him which body they had come to see.

There were approximately eight bodies in there covered with white sheets. They moved to the far right corner of the room.

"This is the one," the coroner said.

He placed some gel under his nose and requested that Jasmine and the officer do the same. The gel was to help kill the scent of death. The smell could add to more traumas, if the stomach is weak. He pulled the sheet back. Jasmine turned and looked at the body. She screamed and couldn't believe that it was Lewis lying there. She ran out of the room, crying hysterically. She had just seen him although not on favorable terms, she still cared about him. The officer came out of the room to look for her. He tried his best to calm her down, but he knew it would take a minute for her to get her thoughts together. From her response, he knew that she recognized him and would be able to help him close out his report. He leaned against the wall waiting patiently for her to calm down, before questioning her about his identity. She finally calmed down and was able to give the officer all the information he needed.

"Ms. Simmons," Sgt Brown said as he turned around.

"Yes!"

"He wanted me to tell you something, before he passed," he said in a very calm voice.

Jasmine said nothing in response, she was hoping it wasn't he loved her.

"He wanted you to know that he was sorry," he said trying not to be dramatic.

"Thank you for everything," Jasmine responded.

They headed out of the hospital, into the parking lot. She thanked him again for his support, and they parted each other's company. Jasmine sat in her car trying to regain her composer. She wanted to get home and lay down; she looked at the time realizing that she had to be at work in a few hours. She knew that there would be no way she was going to be any good to any body tomorrow. She was going to call in and use one of her sick days. Although she wasn't sick now, she knew she would be in the morning. She headed home, before laying down she called Renee.

"Hello! Renee."

"Yes," she responded.

"This is Jasmine, I was just calling to let you know that Lewis was in a terrible car accident," she informed her.

"Oh my goodness is he okay?" she said.

"He was drinking and driving and lost control of his car and ran into a tree. From the amount of alcohol in his system, it prevented him from feeling any pain," she said in a tearful voice.

"I'm so sorry to hear that, did he get a chance to talk to you before he died?" she inquired wondering if she knew why he was over at her place.

"No, I didn't, was he suppose too?" Jasmine responded.

"I was just wondering, again I'm sorry to hear about the accident, I will try and make it to the funeral," she responded.

"Goodnight," Jasmine said as she hung up the phone. She removed her clothes and climbed into bed, she was exhausted and needed some rest. Tomorrow was going to be a stressful day and she needed as much energy as she could get. She laid her head on her pillow, as the final tears of the evening rolled down her face she said, "Give me strength."

CHAPTER 16

Jasmine got up the next morning to find her eyes swollen. She looked in the mirror and wondered if everything was a dream or was yesterday actually a reality. She took her shower and tried to work with her face the best she could, but the swelling around her eyes wasn't cooperating. She called into work using one of her sick days; she knew that she couldn't go in looking as if she was in a boxing match. She picked up the phone wanting to make calls, just to make sure she wasn't dreaming. She first tried Anthony's number, just as before she was greeted by an operator. Again telling her, his number was no longer in service. She then tried Lewis's house, no answer. She tried Renee's number but there was no answer there either, she figured she had left for work already. She checked her caller ID to see what was the last incoming call and just as she feared, it was a number from the hospital. She sat on the bed trying to muster some strength; she was in an emotional crisis. She couldn't locate Anthony; she was betrayed by her best friend and her ex had passed away. She felt bad for hating Lewis, he caused her to hurt one time too many. She was feeling a little guilty, about his accident. She did want him to suffer a little for all the pain he had caused her, but death was not one of her choices. The afternoon came quickly and she had accomplished nothing all morning. She looked out the window to check the weather; she was greeted by raindrops. She heard the postman at the mailboxes making his routine drop.

"I can't believe he's out delivering in this weather," she said to herself.

She figured she'd go and retrieve the mail, which would be her motivation to get out of bed. She opened the box to find it full of mail; she hadn't checked her mailbox in a couple of days. She went back into the apartment, closed the door and sat down at her kitchen table. She fingered through the mail, junk after junk, bill after bill. She came across a letter from Lewis, she looked at the postmark and it was marked for today.

"He must have mailed this last night before the accident," she said to herself.

She put the letter down unable to open it for the fear of what he had to say to her. She wasn't prepared emotionally to read it. She was sure it had something to do with Renee, that's probably why she wanted to know if she had talked to him or not. She tossed the letter on the counter, quickly got dressed and left the apartment. She needed some air and a chance to clear her mind, before she read the letter. Despite the rain, she knew she had to get out of the apartment. She drove around town with no destination in mind, just enjoying the open highway. She pulled off the first exit she came upon, to get some gas. The orange flashing tank was a good indication that she needed to fill up. She filled her tank and ran inside the small convenience store to pay.

While in line she noticed a rack with greeting cards on it, she walked over to the rack to browse through the cards. Her eyes were drawn to a card titled, **"SORRY FOR YOUR LOSS."** She wiped the wetness off her hands before picking up the card and it read...

In this time of grieving, your heart will
start to ache
Holding on to the memories, missing
them you can't fake
When a loved one's body becomes a soul,
we miss them so
Pray they're in God's hands, safe and
that we know
Remember the smiles and the fun you've
shared
In your moments of pain reflect on the
times you really cared
If they left you with pain and agony in
your heart
Forgive them in your prayers allow
yourself a brand new start
Then watch their smiles come shining
down
Feel the rumble in the heavens as they
dance around
Don't reflect on one moment, but their
whole lifetime here
Shed a tear for missing them, then shed
one for good cheer
Let them know you'd have them back no
matter the cost
From our hearts to yours, we are sorry
for your loss

Tears rolled down her cheek as she finished the card, for a moment she was taken out of reality and drawn into the words. She quickly wiped them, before anyone could see them. The card was perfect and fit her heart's thoughts. She wanted a card to send to his family, but she somehow knew that this was a card for her. She paid for her gas, the card and headed back home. Her mind couldn't shake the words of the card. She was caught between the fact that she was hating him before he passed and at one time loving him. She would have him back on earth physically, but not in a relationship with her. She arrived back at her apartment; having no desire to enter knowing that the letter was awaiting her return. She turned the doorknob as if she was unsure of what was on the other side. She made her way over to the letter. She knew she would have to open it, eventually. The evening caught her by surprise. She knew she couldn't put reading it off much longer. She had a couple glasses of wine to help ease her nerves, before opening the letter. She stared at the envelope wondering what he had to say. They're now the words of someone from the dead and that gave her an uneasy feeling. Whatever the letter contained she was now ready, since he took the time out to write it, she would take the time out to read it. She opened the envelope and pulled out the notebook paper it was written on.

She smiled at the letter saying to herself, "He never had good penmanship, sloppy as always."

Dear Jasmine,

Sorry for the formal introduction but I feel like I owed you the truth. The truth about everything that has been going on, that has led up to this moment. First, I would like to say that the contents of this letter will not be pleasant and for that, I say in advance I'm sorry. I can't make up for any of this but when it is all said and done; I want you to know that I love you. If I never get a chance to say it to you, I want to say it to you now that I appreciate everything you've done for me. All that I am today, I am because of you and your support. I want you to be happy and from this day, forward I give you my blessings to move forward. I will no longer get in your way of your pursuit of happiness. You deserve more than I have given you over the last year. I asked God to forgive me for all my sins and all the wrong I have done, so I'm

asking you to forgive me for the things I've done to you. I am in so much pain, my heart is torn into pieces and can't be put back together. I ache at the thought of losing you, but the truth is that I never had you. I loved you from the time I laid eyes on you and wanted to be in your life. I wanted you at any cost, I paid a high price for that, and that was losing you. Well here it goes. I met Renee a couple of months before I met you. We were physically attracted to each other nothing more nothing less. We had a few sexual encounters, and then I saw you and knew that you were the one for me. Renee knew that I was interested in you and she said she would introduce me to you. It came with one stipulation and that was I would have to still give her the sexual attention she needed when she needed it. Yes, you can say I made a pact with the devil. Thinking with my other head I agreed, heck I could have the best of both worlds. Time went by, my love for you grew, and I knew that I couldn't continue the relationship I was having with Renee any longer. When I was trying to break away, she knew my fantasy was to be with two women and that's when Natalie came in the picture. Renee would tell me all the time that you wouldn't go for it and that she could make my fantasy come to life. So she invited me over to her place one evening, you know one of those evenings that I didn't come straight home from work. I was over at her place, having my fantasy come true. I was careless and not thinking at the time, and they started recording the session. The next morning I called her to tell her I couldn't do it, I just wanted you and only you. So she threatened me with the videotape, instead of coming clean I left it alone. Since I wouldn't conform to her wishes, I was set up with Natalie at my job. I guess at this point, they started plotting the destruction of our relationship. Natalie came up a few hours before you showed up, she threw herself at me telling me that she really wanted to be with me. She said that Renee was going to show you the tape that evening. When it was all said and done, you would leave me. She told me that Renee would then have nothing to do with neither one of us. So she threw herself at me and I began to indulge in the moment. I now know that it was a set up, for you to find us together. Renee knew all along that we would be there. Natalie was very persuasive again not thinking I indulged. Hitting Natalie, I now gather, was apart of their plan. Probably, to throw everyone off. I know I hurt you, but I figured that in time, you would forgive me for that. It didn't happen because Renee wouldn't let you live it down, she didn't want us back together. I wanted so much to tell you these things but I didn't know how to. I tried so hard to break away from all of this but I couldn't. Tonight was going to be the last night I was going to be with them. I was going to tell you regardless if she showed you the video or not. I was tired of the secrets and the pain it was causing me. I am telling you all this, because tomorrow is never guaranteed to us. I wanted to make sure that if anything happened to me, you would know the truth and hear it straight from me. I am truly sorry about all this. I was caught up in my own world and never considered you. I was only concerned with my sexual desires and getting them fulfilled. I can say now that the price of having them weren't worth it. I'm sure right now, these words don't mean anything to you, but I love you now and forever more. If this is goodbye, I hope that there's at least one day you could look back on and smile when I cross your mind. Take care of yourself I will now love you from a distance.

Always and forever ,
Lewis

In complete shock she sat back in her chair and felt all her emotions boiling inside her. She started feeling pain, hurt, anger, and sickness in her stomach and most of all hatred for Renee. She wanted so much to go to her house and beat her like the slut she was, but she knew it wouldn't bring Lewis back nor change anything. The damage was done and she had to do what she was doing and that was trying to move on. In a matter of two days, she had lost everything that was dear to her even Lewis. Anthony was gone, her best friend was never her friend and Lewis was dead. She felt herself getting worked up again, she knew that she couldn't take another episode of stress. She fell to her knees to pray before she went to bed, she knew that if anyone could help her right now it would be God.

"Dear God I come to you again this evening to ask you for a favor, I know we had a long conversation last night, but I need to talk to you again. So much has happened and I can't change any of it, I only ask that you allow me to awake out of this nightmare. I know I am nobody special, but if you can hear me I would appreciate it if you could do me this favor, thank you amen," she said as she got off the floor.

She straightened up her place a little then climbed into bed, hoping that God would hear her plea. Calmness came over her as if there was a sign letting her know that everything was going to be okay. She curled up under her comforter and finally was able to fall asleep. As she laid there asleep a smile came across her face as her nightmares were changed to dreams and the vision was soothing to her soul. Her night had ended and she was in her own world.

CHAPTER 17

Jasmine awoke covered in sweat; she sat up in the bed looking around her room to see if there was any sign that her nightmare was true. She turned to the edge of the bed slid on her slippers and began walking down the hallway to the living room. She looked on the counter for the letter Lewis had written her, but it wasn't there. She went into her bathroom to splash some water on her face, to help her wake. For some reason, she didn't feel the same about the dream, something wasn't right. She turned shockingly to the sound of water coming from her shower. It was already running but for some reason, she didn't hear it. She opened the curtain and the sight before her, sent a chill through her spine. He turned and smiled at her, with his well-aligned teeth. His body covered in soap from head to toe and his body parts peeking though the suds.

"What are you doing here?" she said.

"Are you okay? Did you sleep well? You tossed and turned all night long. I tried to wake you but you wouldn't respond" he said as he continued washing off.

"It felt so real," she said as she began to cry. She sat on the closed toilet seat, placed her head in her hands, and wept. He climbed out of the shower suds and all and got down on his knees to give her some comfort. She looked up at him and stared into his eyes.

"What's wrong Jasmine? You're scaring me," he said in a concerned voice.

"I thought I had lost you, I thought you were gone," she said as the tears continued to fall.

He took his hands and rubbed them gently across her face to relieve her skin of the moisture.

"I am real, see," he said as he leaned forward to kiss her on the forehead. She continued to cry and there was no sign of letting up. He helped her onto the floor, wrapped her in his arms and held her until she calmed down. Lying in his arms seemed to have given her some form of comfort; her sniffling and tears had almost instantly come to a halt.

"Talk to me please; tell me what's going on. What did you dream about, that has you so worked up?" he asked.

"I dreamt that I had lost you completely and that I would no longer see you again. Please pinch me let me know I'm awake," she said.

He pinched her and she reacted with a scream, they both laughed at her reactions.

"I guess you are awake now," he said.

"I guess I am," she said.

"Are you alright now? I need to rinse this soap off," he asked.

"I'm sorry, yes please do that," she replied. He stood up and held his hands out to help her off the floor. As he helped her up he pulled her into his arms and stared into her eyes.

"I love you more than life itself and every day that I wake I will love you that much more," he said as he finished his sentence with his lips gently on hers.

He turned and climbed back into the shower, she stood there speechless as his body disappeared behind the shower curtain. Jasmine retreated to her bed to sit down and reflect on her dream. Everything in her was telling her that she was still dreaming; he was not in her shower he couldn't be. The water stopped running and he made his way around the doorway, his body still dripping wet. He dried off in front of her, as she stared at his body wanting to reach out and touch him one more time just to make sure he was real.

"Jasmine you must have been really tired last night," he asked.

"Last night!" she responded with confusion.

"Yes, during the massage I was giving you, you had passed out on the living room floor, so I carried you in here and tucked you in," he said.

Jasmine stared at him not remembering any of these things taking place. She couldn't believe what she was hearing from him.

"So explain to me the robe on the door where did that come from," she asked.

"You don't remember the robe, I gave it to you yesterday as an early birthday gift. I wanted you to have it and after your bath I felt that it would be the right time to give it to you," he said.

"So then what does the initials FM on the robe stand for?" she asked.

"It stands for Frederick Mills the designer, it's from Paris. I'm a little concerned Jasmine, are you sure you're okay?" he asked.

"It's my dream it just seemed so real, I can't explain it all but it all seemed so real," she said.

"What about the dream that isn't real," he asked.

"For starters you," she said as her eyes began to tear up.

"What about me?" he asked.

"You're suppose to be dead, you died in a car accident, I identified the body," she responded with sorrow in her voice. She explained the whole dream to him, the affair he was having with Renee and Natalie, her encounter with Anthony and the accident. He got on his knees in front of her, placed her hands into his.

"You are all I want and will ever need, there's nothing going on between Renee and I now or ever will. You are my world and I will never do anything to destroy my world," he said.

"I do love you Lewis I always have and always will," she responded as tears continued to fall.

"Can I ask you a question?" he asked.

"Sure!" she said.

"Tell me what made you get that tattoo on your back?" he asked.

"Oh! I almost forgot about it, is it healing okay?" she asked as she pulled the bandage off.

"Yes it is, but can you tell me why you got a butterfly?" he asked.

"It represents a new beginning, a struggle from one phase of life to the other. You know like a relationship except in a form of a caterpillar, when it starts out it seems to be doing fine just holding a certain form or understanding. Then one-day things begin to change in the caterpillar/relationship; it takes a turn a new form. Meaning the trials and tribulations begin and for the caterpillar he goes into a cocoon. The thing about cocoons is that they are not attractive at all, when they're in their metamorphic stage. It's changing just like relationships when that stage come, there are only two ways out of it. One the relationship dies in the cocoon phase or two the relationship makes it out of it and blossoms into something beautiful. Like the caterpillar once it makes it out of that phase, it blossoms into a beautiful butterfly. That to me represents us Lewis, we've had our share of difficulties, but in the end our relationship is still standing," she explained.

He hugged her and gave her a kiss. "You're right Jasmine and to prove to you that I will always love you now and forever I have something for you," he said as he walked over to his bag.

He kneeled back down in front of her and again placed her hands into his, "Jasmine you have always been the love of my life even before I met you, I knew that there was someone out there for me and when I saw you I knew it was you."

He pulled out a small box, wrapped in designer wrapping paper. She opened it and as always tears began to fall and she was praying the gift contained what she thought it would. Her eyes lit up at the sight of a two-carrot marquise diamond ring. He held her left hand, placed the ring on the end of her finger, and asked the magic question.

"JASMINE, WILL YOU MARRY ME?"

About G.L.

G.L. Henderson was born as Gregory Lewis Henderson in Tuskegee, AL. He is a successful self-published author, designer, entertainer, and motivational speaker. G.L Henderson's birth into writing romance novels came on Jan 22, 2003 at 3 am. He woke up feeling the urge to express himself and find a vehicle to release all the hurt and pain that was brewing inside him. After going through a devastating year, he had to endure a divorce, the loss of two grand-mothers, two aunts, a best friend and his father. The burdens of life were taking their toll and his writing captures all the emotions and feelings he harbored inside himself. After serving many years of heartaches and joy from past lovers, G.L. has decided to share his experiences with you. You will find yourself drawn into the many characters and story lines. You will feel like he's telling your story or someone's story you know.

For 4 years beginning at the ripe old age of 18, the former U.S. Marine, served as a White House Honor Guard. He served in

Operation Desert Shield and Operation Desert Storm, with the 2nd Marine Division. In 1994, he enlisted in the Army as an Infantryman. In 1996, he volunteered for recruiting duty, where he served as a recruiter, a recruiting station commander, recruiter trainer in the Syracuse Recruiting Battalion and as an instructor at The Army Recruiting and Retention School, at Ft. Jackson, SC.

November 14, 2004, G.L. released his first novel "The Fantasy Master". His first signing was a huge success, selling numerous books that evening, which has also now been released on audio, in a dramatization format. In addition, he has a fashion line called "Camere" which features loungewear for the entire family. With over nine years of experience in recruiting G.L has spoken to hundreds of youths and adults about following their dreams, peer pressure, setting goals and self-motivation. His many speaking engagements include churches, schools, military organizations and youth groups. G.L has toured with local comedians as well as the world Famous Comedy Corner and BET Comic View as an opening act, while marketing his work. G.L is now promoting his own BET Comic view show in

Ft. Knox, KY, while also hosting fashion shows from Washington, D.C, Columbia, SC, Charlotte, NC, Philadelphia and Pittsburgh, PA. G.L has been featured in local newspapers, and has been showcased on news stations in Columbia, SC and Rochester, NY.

G.L. is currently working on his second release "The Illusion of Love", and a third novel "A Child's Cry". In addition, he is working on a book of poetry entitled "From the Heart of G.L.", and a relationship card game. He dedicates his first novel to his daughter Camerie, who he states, "He is her number one fan."

To contact the author
P.O. Box 562765
Charlotte NC, 28256-2765
Email: **glhenderson1@hotmail.com**
Web site: **www.glhenderson.net**

Turn the pages for an exclusive look into the upcoming novel from G.L. Henderson. This is a powerful and compelling story about a young man's lack of patience and understanding for his wife's health situation. This leads him into a world of sexual addiction and the effect it has on everyone around him isn't pleasant…

The Illusion of Love

Coming Soon from G.L.

- ❖ **Audio "The Fantasy Master"**

- ❖ **Clothing Line "Camere"**

- ❖ **"The Illusion of Love"**

- ❖ **Poetry book "From the Heart of G.L. and Friends"**

- ❖ **"A Child's Cry" based on a true story**

The Illusion of Love

CHAPTER 2

The next day came; the light from the morning sun made its way through the cracks in the blinds finding a home on Natasha's face. She turned over to look at her bundle of joy; she smiled as she picked her up. She looked in the crib, but Misty wasn't there. She snatched open the door and ran down the hallway. There she was with Paul; she was in her swing smiling at his funny faces.

"How did you get her, I locked the door last night" she asked.

"It's not like the room is Ft. Knox, I could have come in last night," he responded with a laugh.

"What's happening to you? It seems like you've changed over night," she asked.

"I'm fine there's nothing wrong, don't start with me," he requested.

"I have to get ready for work, why don't you do something with yourself. Ever since the baby, you just don't seem to care much about yourself. You never get your hair or nails done, you're looking rough," he said.

"I can't do those things anymore, you're always complaining about the money and it takes money to do those things" she responded defensively.

He looked at her for a second turned and walked out the door, slamming it behind him. She sat there, placed her head in her hands and cried, his comments pierced her heart. She knew that she had gone through some changes after having the baby. Her hourglass figure had filled out. She no longer had that look he desired. She was stressing out over things she wouldn't normally stress out about. She was unhappy with herself; all of her pre-Misty clothes were too small. She needed a new wardrobe, but she knew they couldn't afford it. She looked over at Misty as she rocked back and forth in her swing. She realized that all of her problems didn't matter, the more she looked at her the happier she became. The telephone rang.

"Hello" Natasha said.

"Hey Tash it's your mom, how are you feeling this morning?" she asked.

"I'm doing fine and yourself?" Natasha responded.

"I was wondering if you wanted to have breakfast with me?" she asked.

"I would mom, but I'm not dressed and Misty isn't either" she responded.

"That's okay I'll come over and help you get her stuff together, I haven't seen you in weeks and besides I want to see my grandbaby," her mom requested.

"We can do breakfast another day," Natasha responded.

"What's really going on? Is there something wrong Tash?" she asked with concern.

"I don't know what's wrong mom, everything is falling apart," she said as her face became instantly covered in tears.

"I'll be right over," she said.

Her mom hung up the phone, gathered her keys and headed over to Natasha's apartment. Natasha sat there, realizing what she had just done. Her mom was against the marriage and she knew that she was going to get the same speech she always gets.

"Leave him you shouldn't have married him in the first place, speech," she said aloud. It was too late she was already on her way over and she had to prepare herself for the criticism she was about to receive. There was a tap at the door.

"Who is it?" Natasha asked.

"It's your mother," she responded.

"Are you sure?" she said as she laughed and opened the door.

She came in gave Natasha a hug and headed over to the baby, who had fallen asleep in her swing.

"She is so precious looks like she's gaining weight, have you been giving her table food? Look at this house, looks like a tornado touchdown here. I know I raised you better than this?" her mother asked as she sat on the sofa.

"I know mom it's rough around here raising Misty, worrying about money and Paul," she said as she sat on the sofa next to her mom.

"Honey you have to get yourself together you can't let that man worry you, like this. You have a child to raise, now you have to put all that other stuff aside," she said to Natasha.

"It's easier said than done," she responded.

"What exactly is he doing that's driving you crazy?" she asked.

Natasha knew that if she told her what happened, her mom would never like him. If she didn't tell her she was going to bug her until she was satisfied with the story.

"Mom I believe Paul is going to cheat on me, if he hasn't already done so," she said.

"Why would you say that?" she asked.

"He's been hanging out late at night, I know he's been at the gentlemen's club. He has been using our money to buy adult tapes and I'm sure he's spending money at that club" she said as she got up and pulled one out of the VCR.

"Mmm, Mmm, Mmm," her mom said shaking her head in disappointment.

"He's been masturbating a lot, he doesn't lay next to me anymore. He calls me hurtful names, he says I'm fat and out of shape. He won't leave money for me to get my hair done. His clothes smell like cigarettes and perfume. If he isn't cheating now, he will soon. I hate my body, I don't want him to touch me, because I know he's not touching me for me. He's only touching me because he's horny," she said with concern in her voice.

"You're more than that, Tash you're a precious jewel and you can't let anyone, especially a man make you feel less than what you are. I told you not to marry him in the first place it was too fast. I want you to be happy, this is not being happy," she said as she looked around the apartment.

"He's a good man mom, I know he loves me and I love him despite how we got married. He's just going through something and I don't want to abandon him, no matter how much it hurts me," she said in his defense.

"Well I hope you know what you're doing. There are some good men out there so I wish you would leave him. I'm sure you can find someone who would treat you right," her mom said.

"Mom just because someone may be perfect to you, doesn't make him my Mr. Right," she said.

"Tash I just don't want to see you hurt, you're my child no matter how grown you think you are. No matter what man is in your life I will always be there for you?" she said.

She wrapped her arms around her and held Natasha tight, the more she held her the more Natasha's emotions brewed.

"Mom why does love hurt so much? I thought being married would eliminate the pain. Why is he doing these things, why is he hurting me so? I can't sleep at night, I can't eat, all I think about is him," she said as tears rolled down her face.

Her cries were piercing her mother's heart; she knew she needed her arms not her words.

"It' okay baby everything will work out, shhh! Stop crying you're going to make yourself sick," she said to Tash.

Natasha tried to stop crying but the more she thought about Paul the more she cried, her heart was far from healing. She wanted so much to remove the pain, she wanted to ball up and die.

"I love him more than words can say, I just want the pain to go away," she said.

"It will baby just keep praying and ask God to fix your family I know he will," she said to her.

Wiping her tears she asked her mom, "When did you become religious?"

"I'm not, but I do know that he can help you, I believe that much," she replied.

She laughed, "I'm sure he can".

"I just want to have a normal family, I want him to know that I love him and I will do anything for him," she said.

"Baby you first have to get yourself together, let him know that you can make it with or without him. As long as he knows you have to depend on him, he'll continue doing what he wants," she said to her.

"I know mom, but I…," she began to say before being interrupted by the phone.

"Hello," she asked.

"Hey Tash I was calling to let you know, I'll be hanging out with the guys after work for a little while. So don't wait up for me okay," he said.

"Don't do this again why can't you just come home and be with us," she begged.

"Don't start throwing that guilt trip on me, I just want time to myself you know some of us do work," he responded.

"Taking care of Misty is a full time job in itself, you do know who she is don't you?" she sarcastically responded.

"Very funny," he said.

"What about food? There's none in the house." she asked.

"I'm sure there's something in there you can whip together for yourself, I'll get something while I'm out," he said.

"Paul can you please come home," she continued to beg.

"Let me talk to him," her mom said as she reached for the telephone.

"No mom I can handle this," she said.

"Oh! I guess you've been putting our business out in the streets again," he said.

"No! It's not like that," she responded.

"Sure it isn't, bye Tash see you later," he said.

"Paul don't," she said as the phone hung up in her face.

"Paul! Paul!" she screamed into the phone.

"I told you to let him go Tash he's no good," her mom said.

"Stop talking like that, we're going to work it out," she said.

"Wake up child, see the light. He *is* a man," she said.

"What's that suppose to mean?" she asked.

"He's going to keep treating you like this until he runs you into the ground," she said.

"So if I leave him who's to say the next man won't be worst," she asked.

"I'm just sure there's someone who will treat you better," she replied.

"I'm sure there is someone, in the beginning they all treat you right. Tell you all the things you want to hear, do all the things you want them to do. They are always better than the last guy; until they reach the point of ownership then the true person comes out. Well, I have grown to know him and the things he does, so I am willing to work with what I got. I know we can make it, I know he can change," she said.

"Look around you sweetie, look at this place tell me what do you see? I see an apartment filled with confusion, hurt and pain. You're too young to be going through this; I just don't want you to hate men like I do. Your dad put me through a lot and he scarred me for life. He cheated and ran the streets, he was a good provider but he loved the streets. That was entirely too much for me to handle. I just don't want you to end up like me, alone," she said with sadness in her eyes.

"Mom you chose to be by yourself, you and dad could have worked it out. I am going to give this my all, remember these words until death do us part. Mom I can make it through this, so every time something comes up should I run?" she asked.

"I'm just saying that you could be doing better, you know they're talking about your marriage in the streets?" she replied.

"Now the truth comes out, this isn't about me this is about you. You're worried about what people are saying," she asked her mother in anger.

"I'm getting tired of hearing the gossip about my child," she said.

"I don't care about those people and what they think, this is my house and what goes on in here is my business," she said aggressively.

There was a long silence as they sat there, looking at each other like boxers waiting for the bell to ring.

"Well let me go get some groceries for you I'll make dinner for you, I'll drop it off later," she said as she gathered her things.

"Thanks for everything mom," she said as she hugged her.

"No problem just try and stay strong, remember show him you can make it with or without him, I love you Tash," she said as she returned the hug.

"I love you too mom," she said as she watched her mom walk down the hall.

She closed the door and looked at her place and realized she needed to do some cleaning. She turned on the radio and began cleaning and thinking about the conversation that took place between her and her mom. She knew she was right about a few things, but giving up her family wasn't one of them. Trying not to think about it she went back to doing her work. Hoping that Paul decided to come home and not go out.